A WENDIGO INVITES US TO DINNER

~

I SPOKE TO THE GUARD OF HADES

A Lore Series - 1

CREATED BY Sy S. Kanaan

A WENDIGO INVITES US TO DINNER

I SPOKE TO THE GUARD OF HADES

CONTENTS

STORY 1:

A WENDIGO INVITES US TO DINNER

I wasn't always thrilled by roadtrips. Ever since I was young, when my parents would take me on trips outside of my hometown, I would often get car sickness at some point along the way. I eventually grew out of that, but even as I got older, my distaste for the long hours of traffic jams and being in the same seat all day hadn't gone away.

I'm grown now, and my girlfriend, Sahrye, was fond of going on trips. Ever since we'd been dating during our early college years, she had been telling me about how much she longed to explore the outdoors. The thing is, when she said "outdoors," she didn't just mean going on long walks in the park or simple bird watching. Think of your stereotypical bungee-jumping, back-flipping into a community lake, daredevil type of girlfriend. That was my Sahrye.

Now, most people would wonder how an adventurous chick like her would match up with someone like me, a person who prefers the security of their own home and the familiarity of the city they reside in. Most people would think of me as the exact opposite of an adventurous risk taker. Honestly, I wish I knew why we were so inseparable yet so different in tastes and activities. We first met at a library where I spent most of my freetime in college, even when I wasn't studying. Other than reading and debating people on online forums, my recreational time would otherwise be spent on video games, which just so happened to be an activity we both enjoyed. So when I first asked her out in the library, I asked for her gamer tag and we played online and talked for a while. Before I knew it, we were a couple.

Of course, it was just a matter of time before I had to respect Sahrye's desires to go on more adventurous activities, even if it meant leaving my shell. Honestly, despite not being into leaving my hometown to go on strange and dangerous trips, I didn't have any regrets as long as she was with me. For the past two years, Sahrye used her sweet, persuasive voice to talk me into going on the most bizarre trips I'd never imagined myself doing. For example, last year we went off-road racing in Moab, Utah, where we rented a couple of UTVs and drove around in the dry, rocky desert region. A wild bumpy ride across sand, rocks, and hills was insane enough for me, but it wasn't enough for Sahrye. She urged me to race with her at top speeds through the rest of the trail. The guide who rode with us advised against it, but before we knew it, we were both driving at top speeds in the dirt, laughing while our heads and bodies bounced around in our jeeps as we blasted across the trail.

There was also a time when we went fishing in the Everglades, which I thought would be a fun experience until I learned that the waters had pythons and alligators. When I found my fishing line entangled with a large black snake, my soul nearly left my body. Luckily, the snake managed to free itself from the line and slithered back into the water. Sahrye noted that the snake wasn't even venomous and was likely more afraid of me than I was of it. We had a damn good laugh that day.

It was adventures like these that strengthened our bond and eventually broke me away from my disdain of traveling. So when me and Sahrye decided it was time for a new adventure, I came up with the idea to go on a road trip into Montana. There was a hot springs resort that I'd been looking at online. The hotels in the area had decent pools, large clean rooms, and plenty of activities for us to enjoy, like horseback riding and hiking. *It's the perfect trip idea*, I thought at first. However, when I brought the idea up to her, she almost reluctantly revealed a detail that she'd forgotten to include. She wanted to invite her childhood friend, Clare and her fiancé, Wyatt. Now, don't get me wrong, I didn't mind having extra companions on our trips, although we had never actually done that before. But as I mentioned, the trip was meant to help me and her bond, not to share the experience with other people, especially those whom I'd never met. I gave it some thought and after looking into her sparkling, brown, pleading eyes, I folded.

The next thing I knew, there I was piled into a large rental van with Sahrye, Clare and Wyatt, who drove most of the way. According to Google, the ride was a little over twelve hours, with plenty of mountainous roads and forests along the way. We decided to take turns driving until we were all too tired to drive and then one of us would look for a motel to sleep at until the next morning. I started the first three and a half hours of driving, getting us out of the early morning traffic of Aurora, Colorado.

Sahrye took the wheel for an hour before we stopped for lunch at a diner in central Wyoming. Afterward, Wyatt took the wheel and knocked out a good five hours while Clare volunteered as the van's DJ. She selected through her playlists which, I hate to admit, I actually enjoyed most of the time. Other than that, we all chatted about our lives, our hobbies, and everything we had to look forward to once we arrived in Montana. After Wyatt managed to knock off five hours of driving, we all looked to Clare to take her turn at the wheel. Unfortunately, according to her, she was too fatigued from staying awake the whole time DJing.

We spent that evening looking for a motel that was cheap enough to not make a dent in our travel budget, yet had a decent rating that didn't mention anything about murders, theft, or credit card scams being common in the area. Sahrye managed to find one motel that was a little over fifty bucks a night, which was just enough for us to split and pay for together. We ended up getting one room with two beds. Clare inspected the sheets and said they looked clean enough to sleep in, meaning there were no visible blood or shit stains anywhere. At one point, Wyatt went to check inside the small fridge underneath the television stand. He looked briefly at the girls, who were busy conversing as they dug around through their bags. He then turned to me and whispered, "Hey, Aaron."

I turned and noticed he made a slight head motion, telling me to check out something in the fridge. I calmly made my way over and looked inside and was grossed out by what we found. It was a large cockroach that seemed to be squashed and smeared in its own remains and gunk. A blob of legs, wings, and brown slime was in the center of the bottom of the fridge. I took a piece of tissue and wiped up the dead bug and flushed it down the toilet. Me and Wyatt agreed to not let the girls know about what we found, and to make sure all of our bags remain closed for the rest of the night.

After ordering some wings and fries and a few sodas, we ate and went straight to bed. Wyatt and Clare almost immediately fell asleep as their heads hit the pillow, while me and Sahrye stayed up for a little while longer. Sahrye looked at her phone while I swiped away on mine, gazing at social media. Suddenly, Sahrye sucked her teeth and said, "Fuck!"

"What's up?" I asked, concerned and low-key hoping she hadn't found a roach crawling on the bed. Although she was usually the brave one during our trips, she was usually the first to leave the room at the sight of a roach or a spider. When I looked over at her, her eyes were still glued to her phone screen, but I knew from the worried expression on her face that something was definitely wrong.

"The forecast says there's a snow storm coming from the northwest," she said disappointed. "At least five to six inches by noon." She tilted the phone toward me so I could see. Sure enough, the screen showed a map of Wyoming and Montana being engulfed in a wave of blue, indicating that a large mass of wintry storms was heading our way. I noticed the time of expectancy was showing that the storm would be on our route by noon the next day.

"We got plenty of time," I said, turning my phone off and turning over to sleep.

"I don't know, Aaron," Sahrye sighed. "This storm looks like it's gonna be nasty. Maybe we should chill here for an extra night. We got the money, and I know Clare and Wyatt won't mind."

"Or…we can just get up a little early, beat the storm, and check in at the resort just as the storm touches down." My eyes were closed when I made my suggestion, but I could tell by Sahrye's silence that she had doubts about my plan.

We all woke at the crack of dawn and I spoke with Clare and Wyatt about the storm. They were hesitant at first, but after learning that we were only a few hours from our destination, they agreed with my plan to leave early. Wyatt offered to drive the remaining hours, since he was better at driving long distances than the rest of us. I told him I didn't mind and that I would take the wheel as soon as he got tired.

The road was dry that morning and the traffic was moderate, so my plan to make it to the resort seemed like it would go smoothly. That all changed only an hour later. The trouble started when we received alerts on the GPS about an accident involving two cars and an eighteen-wheeler. Apparently one of the four wheelers switched lanes at the worst time possible and collided with another car. Worse, the second car abruptly braked upon collision while a semi-truck drove behind it. Then the semi crashed against the second vehicle, causing it to lose control and crash into the median. The alerts warned that the delay would take hours to get through.

Clare began looking up new routes to go around the five-mile traffic jam that followed the accident. She found one that would add another hour to our drive but would allow us to avoid the traffic jam before it got worse. The route was an old highway with very few fuel stops and towns, but we all agreed it was the only alternative to being stuck on the interstate.

Wyatt switched the route on the GPS and followed an exit off the interstate toward the alternate route. Worry began to set in when the clouds started to thicken and the GPS directed us to a dense wooded road with two lanes. We noticed the fewer number of cars that passed us. Eventually, it was like we were the only travelers on the road for miles. Just as anxiety got a hold of us all, snow began to fall. At first, there were a few gusts of flurries that brushed gently along the van's windshield and disappeared. Then we were met with a white mass that looked like a wall. Wyatt gently pressed the brakes as the wall of snow swallowed us.

Clare told Wyatt to turn his high beams on, although they were no match for the incoming barrage of snow that blasted the van. Ice and slush accumulated along the sides of the windshield and the windows. I sat in the back seat next to Sahrye, who looked outside at the clumps of ice that grew on the window, blocking the view. I looked forward to the windshield. Although Wyatt tried his best to look calm, I could tell by his slight, jerky hand motions that he struggled to keep the van in the lane. The road was completely white now, and it was impossible to tell if it was still two lanes.

"Slow down, babe," Clare cried nervously. Wyatt looked on and ignored her as he tried to keep the van steady. The winds continued to howl and pick up, pushing and rocking the van as we rode down the winding path through the woods.

Suddenly Wyatt yelled, "Shit!" before braking abruptly. Clare yelped as she held to her seat. I felt the van skid for a moment before it finally stopped in the road.

"Wyatt," I called out, "what's going on?" He said nothing, but I could hear him breathing heavily as he looked in front of him. To our dismay, a massive snow-covered tree lay across the center of the road. Broken branches and shattered chips proved that the incident just happened.

"We can't stay here," Sahrye said with a quiver in her voice. She sounded genuinely scared and I didn't blame her. I gently reached over for her hand and closed mine around it. It was shaking. Alot. I held it firmly to reassure her and I called up to the front seat.

"H-hey, maybe we should turn around." I realized I was stammering, which meant my suggestion wasn't convincing at all.

Sahrye pulled out her phone and began typing. "There's gotta be a safe way back. I'm looking for another route."

I started to pull out my phone when something caught my attention from the corner of my eye. I turned toward a bright light coming behind the van. It was a pair of headlights coming straight for us at top speed. I immediately grabbed Sahrye and yelled, "Get out of the car! Now!"

My instincts urged me to drag Sahrye and myself out of the car, but it was too late. Just as soon as I screamed, the other car swerved and crashed into the back of us at an angle that forced us to slide over the edge of the road. All four of us screamed as the van tumbled into the woods. Snow, grass, tree branches, and rocks collided with the windshield. I heard the metal crumble, squeak, and groan as it rolled on through the thicket. I could hear Sahrye scream as she held onto me. I could hear Clare pray and swear while Wyatt lost the grip of the wheel and began to bobble and sway in his seat. During all of this, all I could think was that all of this was all my fault.

"Aaron! Aaron!" Someone yelled my name and fiercely shook me by my shoulders. I forced my eyes open and focused on the blurry person in front of me. It was Sahrye. Her eyes were full of tears that dropped on my face as she screamed my name. As my vision came into focus, I saw dirt smudges on her cheeks and small scars scattered across her arms. I struggled, trying to sit upright, and my head began to hurt severely.

Sahrye gasped and held my shoulders to keep me from falling back. "Oh my god. Are you okay? You can hear me right? Can you say something?"

I nodded, somewhat hoping that'd answer most of her questions. I looked around slowly, still enduring the migraine. "Others?" I asked with strain.

Sahrye pointed behind me. I turned and saw Wyatt, who was kneeling next to Clare. I managed to stand up and staggered slowly towards the couple. I sighed in relief when I saw that Clare was still breathing, although she was doing so in a heavy and frantic manner. Tears streamed down her face and she screamed in agony as Wyatt moved his hands around the center part of her body. I approached closer and saw that Clare's arm was bent at a wrong angle. Wyatt was gently holding the arm while looking at it. He looked back at Clare for a brief second with guilt. She was still screaming and praying. Wyatt turned back to the broken arm and slowly held it up. Then, with a swift switch of his hands, he snapped the bones back in place. This was when Clare bellowed loud enough for the woods to let the scream echo for miles.

Sahrye was now crouching beside her, shushing her and whispering to her to calm her down. Wyatt, who later made it known that he was a medical student at a university back home, was aligning the bone with a splint he made and secured with a small tree branch and a piece of cloth he had ripped from the bottom of his shirt. Unfortunately, we didn't have a first aid kit or any ointment or medicine, so whatever pain Clare felt, she had to endure it until we returned to society.

I decided to stand up and look around us. The storm seemed to have stopped a while ago, but only after covering up the tire tracks of the runaway van that was now lying on its side against a tree. There was no trail or tracks to follow back to the highway. Our phones were now useless. Both me and Clare lost our phones during the crash, Sahrye's phone had run out of charge, and Wyatt's phone was completely broken.

After getting Clare to her feet, we all debated on how we were getting back to society. We were at the center of a snowy forest with a steep slope above us. We all agreed that we obviously slid down this slope after the collision, therefore the road must be on the top of the hill. Our only way out of the forest was up. The only question was how long would we have to scale the slope and in which direction, especially since one of us was injured?

The sun was starting to set so we decided to go to the van and gather enough supplies and clothes to stay warm for the night. We decided to continue up the slope in the morning since moving around in the woods at night was too risky, dark, and cold. Luckily there weren't any signs of another storm coming, but the temperature wasn't getting any higher. It was my idea to bring two coats and extra clothes. Now both me and Sahrye wore as many layers as we felt we needed to stay warm. Wyatt took some branches and used a lighter to start a fire for us to sit around to both keep us warm and to keep nocturnal animals from coming too close to us.

We sat for the rest of the night trying to register our entire situation. Wyatt continued to try to activate his broken phone with no luck. His frustrated attempts to get the phone to respond were met with a glitchy, shattered screen. I was certain my phone was somewhere in the thickets on the hill. Clare tried her best to keep her arm elevated and the bandage and twig in place. She was no longer screaming or whimpering as she was before, but she was now pale after enduring the pain and trauma from the crash. Sahrye sat next to me and stared blankly into the fire.

The cold night of awkward silence and a throbbing headache was bad enough, but something else was off. You know that paranoid feeling that you're being watched? I felt that. It happened later in the night when I noticed Sahrye nodded off and fell asleep on my shoulder. Wyatt sat awake while Clare closed her eyes and lay across his lap. Occasionally I would peer into the woods around us and see nothing but darkness. I imagined that a deer or a fox or something was eyeing us from the shadows. I shrugged it off after a few head turns to make sure there wasn't something large and hungry lurking. Then again, as long as the fire kept burning, I figured that was enough to keep predators away. That reassuring thought was enough to convince me to fall into a light sleep.

"Get your fucking hands off me!"

I jolted awake at the sound of one of the women screaming. I looked up and realized it was Sahrye who was screaming at the top of her lungs. She was standing face to face with Wyatt who was yelling back. "You gotta calm down! You're loud for no reason! I already answered you!"

This was when I had to intervene. There's something about watching your girlfriend argue with a guy you just met a couple days ago, but for it to happen in the middle of the woods at night was a situation I couldn't let escalate. I walked in between them and asked what was going on.

"I don't know," Sahrye said angrily. "Ask him what the problem is. Tell him what you told me, Wyatt."

I turned to Wyatt, who was now pulling on his own hair in frustration and had tears in his eyes. Now I knew something fucked up just happened. "Wyatt?" I asked, hoping he would calm down before answering.

Sniffling, Wyatt struggled to respond and stuttered, "I-I was sleeping and she was…she was right here. I got up to take a leak, dude. I swear I was only a few feet away. And then. And then…I-I don't know what happened! That's all I know!" Tears streamed down his face as he tried to talk. I'd only met the guy a couple of days ago and I never imagined he could become so distraught.

"Wyatt! Just tell me what's going on," I demanded, both tired and agitated now.

Sahrye then interrupted and said, "Clare is gone."

"What?" I tried repeating her words in my head to make sure I heard her right. That was when it dawned on me that Clare was no longer laying down. The last time I saw her, she was lying on Wyatt's lap, and now she had vanished.

"I already told you, "Wyatt snapped. "She was lying next to me when I woke up to take a whiz. I turned around and she was just gone."

"Well, I didn't see her," Sahrye said. "All I know is that I woke up and I saw that she was gone and you were walking back without her. Who else could she have gone with?"

"Are you implying that I did something to MY fiancée?"

"I just want to know what you did with MY best friend. She couldn't have just got up and left by herself. That's just not her." As Sahrye spoke, she became more confrontational and accusatory, but I understood her anger. It was late at night and we were in the middle of nowhere. Clare didn't seem like the type to do something as dumb as running out in the dark on her own.

"When did all this happen?" I asked.

Wyatt shook his head. "Barely five minutes ago, maybe."

"It was at least ten!" Sahrye snapped

"There's no fucking clocks out here, Sahrye!"

"I knew there was something off about you, Wyatt. You know what? Clare told me you were always doing sneaky shit. Coming home late and shit. And what about that time you cheated on her? You thought I didn't know about that?"

Wyatt threw his hands up in frustration and disbelief. "That was over a year ago. And what the fuck does that have to do with this?"

Sahrye pointed her finger towards his face and made a silencing motion. "It shows that you are a liar and she had absolutely no reason to trust you. Now get the fuck out of my face!"

She walked to the edge of the darkness of the woods and screamed for Clare. She did this a couple times and waited. No response. In fact, there was no sound at all. It was as if the forest was mute. It could've been because it was wintertime and all the crickets and frogs weren't around this time of year. But the silence seemed…unnatural.

I looked around into the darkness when I noticed something glistening in the firelight. There were red droplets scattered along a trail of human-sized footprints leading into the forest. The drops were still seeping into the snow, which means they were fresh. Very fresh. I choked when my first thought passed through my mind. I pointed to the trail of red droplets and both Sahrye and Wyatt dropped their jaws and gasped.

Wyatt yelled, "Clare!" He then ran to the van and reached into his luggage. He ran back toward us with a flashlight and followed the thin trail of blood into the woods.

I tried to call back for him to wait for us, but by then he was gone. Sahrye went into our luggage and pulled out a pair of flashlights that we always brought just in case of an emergency. Immediately we began to follow Wyatt and his light into the woods, uncertain what we'd find. But we had to at least look. I mean, getting out of this mess was gonna be difficult enough, but going back home and explaining to everyone about our friend's disappearance would be worse.

Wyatt began to slow down eventually after walking for what seemed like minutes. I looked back for a moment and noticed that the fire near the wreckage was going low.

"The flame is starting to die out," I mentioned to Sahrye.

She turned and noticed what I was talking about. "Yeah. Don't worry about that. We'll just follow our tracks back."

"Right," I responded. After hearing that, I realized something. "Hey, do you know Clare's shoe size?"

Sahrye stopped for a moment to think. Then she said, "Five, I think. Why?"

I immediately stopped to look at the tracks. I was too tired to notice at first, but the tracks didn't show any tread marks in the snow like mine, Sahrye's, or Wyatt's. They were human-sized, but they definitely weren't a size five. They were large, heavy indentations, like someone tall and massive were trudging through the snow. I noticed the specks of blood were no longer showing in the snow, but as I thought about that, another gruesome possibility popped into mind.

"Sahrye. This might be a reach. But I think there's someone else here. Someone might have Clare. And when I say they have her, I mean they might be *carrying* her."

Sahrye looked at the tracks and realized what I was saying. Whoever made these tracks couldn't have been Clare. Clare was a short and thin woman, and these prints were left by a taller individual who had no tread on their footwear. In fact, the closer I looked at them, the more they looked almost hoof-shaped but I figured that was impossible since the tracks were made with two legs. *Were they riding on a horse?* I thought, just before shaking the absurd idea from my head. There's no way someone would ride around horseback in the woods at this time of night.

When me and Sahrye agreed that there was most likely another person walking in the woods with us, we tried to call out to Wyatt. However, it was no use. He was too far ahead. I could barely see his flashlight bounce around as he jogged ahead of us. The woods were getting thicker now, and the longer we walked, the more difficult it'd be to find our way back to the wreck.

"Wyatt!" I yelled but got no response. Within moments of walking farther, we couldn't even see his flashlight anymore. This was bad.

"Great," Sahrye sighed. "I think we lost the tracks. The first ones, I mean. I can see Wyatt's, but the others are gone."

I looked down at the tracks and realized there was now only one set in the snow. It was Wyatt's. That meant we must've just lost the trail recently while we were calling out to him.

"We're going too far," I added. I raised my hand up and yelled, "Clare! Wyatt!"

Me and Sahrye stopped and waited for someone to respond. Then Sahrye began to cup her hands around her mouth to call out the names again. That was when we heard it.

Something screamed. I mean really loud. And when I say *something*, I mean that whatever made the scream couldn't have possibly been human. Not only did it seem to be abrupt and loud, but something about it was unnatural. It was the sound of wailing or a shriek. It was full of pain and rage. Worst of all, it wasn't far.

It reminded me of the high-pitched callings that elks make to each other in the wild but this sounded too distorted and almost monstrous to be an elk. It almost sounded like a predatory creature was calling to intimidate its prey.

"Aaron," Sahrye whispered, "I don't like this." For the first time, since I'd known her, she actually looked frightened. She was literally the bravest and most daring person I knew, but even she was losing her cool in this situation. I didn't blame her. I'd lost my cool since the wreck, but after we entered the dark woods, we were dealing with snow, tall trees, mysterious footprints and crazy animals yelling in the distance. I hated to admit it, but I was ready to turn back.

Me and Sahrye looked at each other for a moment, almost as though we were thinking the same thing. We started to turn away reluctantly when we saw something bright bounce ahead of us. We both turned again and saw Wyatt coming toward us with his light in his hand. We were almost relieved to see him again…until we saw that a large piece of his coat was missing.

No, wait, I thought. I looked closer at him as he ran in our direction. His coat was ripped to shreds on one side. I saw five long gashes along the front of his abdomen and stomach, spilling blood as he ran with a limp. His face was twisted with pain and terror.

"Run! Get the fuck out of here!" His clothes were soaked with his own blood. Me and Sahrye began to run back to the wreckage as Wyatt ran behind us. I didn't dare ask what he was running from. Judging from the wound, I definitely didn't want it to catch up to the rest of us.

Sahrye called back to Wyatt and asked,"Wyatt! Did you find Clare?!"

He didn't answer. He was breathing too heavily with panic, but he forced himself to say,"Keep going! Don't stop!"

We did just that. We ran until we made it to the wreckage. The fire was a pile of embers now, but we were still able to see the van. I opened the side door and helped Sahrye inside before I started to crawl into it. I watched as Wyatt ran for us and I held the door open for him. I wish I hadn't.

It all happened in the blink of an eye. Wyatt was barely a full yard away when I noticed the thing that was chasing him was closing in on him. At first, I couldn't make out what it was. It was a shadowy mass that ran on all fours in a frenzied, galloping motion like a rampaging bear. Then I saw that the skin of the animal didn't only have fur, but patches of bone and rotting flesh showed through its hide. I saw how thin it was; a body with ribs nearly bursting through its own skin. That wasn't the most disturbing part. The feature that nearly stopped my heart was its face. It was all bone. The creature's head resembled that of a large deer skull, with antlers swinging side to side as it ran directly behind Wyatt. From a distance, you would think it was wearing a mask, but from the way its jaws opened and snapped as the creature huffed and groaned, it was apparent that that wasn't a mask at all.

I was petrified with horror as I watched the creature descend upon Wyatt, who was already weakened from his wounds and the long run afterwards. In a quick motion, the creature arched its back and pounced on Wyatt's back, pushing its large, black claws into his spine. The claws were similar to those of a sloth, only there were five long black talons that pierced into Wyatt's flesh. The creature gave him no time to scream as he reared his bony head back and bit down into his neck, crushing and tearing into his windpipe. The monster twisted its neck around as it worked its jagged molars into the flesh, making a violent cracking sound.

I forced myself to crawl into the van and slammed the door shut, locking it instantly. Sahrye looked at me with wide shocked eyes and asked,"What was it? Where's Wyatt?"

She didn't see it, I realized. She didn't see what Wyatt was running from, or what happened to him. How could I tell her that one of her friends was literally getting devoured as we sat in the van? How could I tell her that that horrible monster probably took Clare away in the first place?

The closed van door blocked the sounds of the large, skull-faced creature ripping into Wyatt. I knew that if it saw me and Sahrye enter the van, it would eventually come over to investigate. Instinctively, I searched the van for something to defend ourselves with.

Sahrye watched in confusion as I tore through our luggage. Then I rummaged through Clare and Wyatt's bags, hoping to find a knife or a gun or something. To my surprise, I reached into a bag and felt something hard. I wrapped my hand around the object to find that it was a handle of something small and heavy. It felt like a gun. I pulled the object out and I was correct. It was a six-round revolver and I recognized that the bag once belonged to Wyatt. If he had survived a little longer, he would've run straight for this pistol to defend himself.

Sahrye grabbed my shoulder when she saw what I was looking at. "Aaron. Stop ignoring me! What's going on! Where did you get that?"

I couldn't answer her. Not yet. I opened the chamber to see that there were only four rounds inside. I was sure Wyatt might've had a box of extra bullets somewhere in his bag, but I knew we didn't have time.

"Aaron!" Sahrye was screaming louder now. Too loud, I realized. I turned to her and placed my hand over her mouth to silence her, only for her to push me away and scream louder.

"Why aren't you answering me? What the fuck is going on? Where are they?"

"Shut up," I whispered harshly.

She froze and stared at me in shock. She lowered her voice, but it wasn't anywhere close to a whisper. "What are you doing? Why do you have a gun?"

I realized I couldn't hide the truth from her anymore. Something inside me snapped, and before I could hinder myself, I yelled, "They're dead, Sahrye! Both of them!"

Her blank stare said it all. She couldn't believe me. She didn't WANT to believe me, but I could see from her tearing eyes that a wave of realization and sadness was rushing over her. Wyatt wasn't coming back and Clare's whereabouts were still a mystery. I hated to admit it, but I knew that if she was still out there, the creature would've taken her.

Sahrye was now holding her head in her hands, freaking out while trying to piece together everything that was happening.

"W-what's going on? Why is this happening?" She shivered as she spoke, like a mental health patient on the verge of a nervous breakdown. I couldn't bear to keep her in the dark anymore. I had to tell her something.

"Th-there is…something out there," I stammered. "Something is hunting us."

Sahrye's eyes widened. "Is it a bear?"

I shook my head. I didn't know what that thing was. All I knew was that it was still out there. For a while, we sat in silence. The windows were covered in ice and dirt, so it was impossible to see outside. To soothe my discomfort, I sat close to Sahrye, hoping to help keep her warm as we waited until morning. She didn't say much and I could tell she was still eyeing the gun that I had partially sitting in my coat pocket. I knew she hated guns, but there wasn't a chance in hell I was gonna leave it out of arm's reach.

We sat there for what felt like an eternity. I considered peeking out the door to see if the creature was out there. Suddenly, just as the thought passed, me and Sahrye jumped at the sound of something hammering from the outside of the van. I immediately picked up the revolver and aimed it towards the direction of the sound. It was on the other side of the door. Someone or something wanted to get in. Through the frost and filth coated windows, all we could see was a silhouette of something standing in front of the door.

"Hello," a small, weak voice called. "Is someone there? Wyatt?"

Me and Sahrye turned to each other in shock. It sounded like Clare. "Clare?" Sahrye cried.

"Sahrye," Clare's voice replied. "Are you alright?"

I slowly moved to the door and slid it open. Clare was pale, her hair was tangled, and her skin and clothes had more dirt smudges than before. When she saw us, she cried and hurriedly climbed inside, closing the door immediately behind her. We couldn't believe it, but she was alive.

Once she was inside the van with us, she and Sahrye hugged and cried together for a long moment.

"Where were you?" Sahrye asked. "We thought you died."

"Died?" Clare repeated.

"You disappeared and we saw a trail of blood," I added.

"My arm," she said, lifting her bandaged arm up. "The wound opened up. I got up after Wyatt went to pee. That was when I noticed my arm was bleeding again. Wyatt wiped it earlier and told me not to bother it, but I wanted to make sure, so I unwrapped it a little to look at it."

We looked at her bandage. It was almost soaked with blood. I felt horribly guilty and almost regretted not just hiking up the hill to get help when we still had daylight.

"I didn't know how to stop the bleeding and the splint fell apart so I went to look for Wyatt when–"

She stopped abruptly, as if she wasn't sure if she should say what she wanted to say next. A wave of uncertainty and fear flashed across her face.

"When what?" asked Sahrye.

"I saw something. Or I thought I saw something following me when I walked around looking for Wyatt. At first, all I heard was some footsteps in the snow, but it sounded distant. Then it sped up like it was right behind me. This might've been stupid, but I just ran. I ran farther than I thought I could, with a broken arm and all, but I just didn't want to look back."

I thought about the big footprints in the snow earlier. I realized that I was right about them. They weren't Clare's. Someone, or something, was following her. I was willing to bet it was the monster from earlier, but I waited to see if Clare would mention it.

"So I kept running and running," she continued. "Then everything around me was getting darker and darker. I couldn't hear the footsteps behind me by then, but I turned around and realized I was lost. Luckily, I was able to trace my steps and found you guys. I wish you or Wyatt would've rebuilt the fire though. It definitely would've helped."

She doesn't know, I realized. I looked at Sahrye, who looked back at me nervously, then back at Clare. I took a deep breath and asked her, "Clare, did you see something out there? That thing that was chasing you. Did you see…it?"

She gave me a blank stare. "See it? No, I didn't see anything. I just heard something and had a bad feeling. That's all. It probably wasn't anything. It was my imagination. I was just losing my mind after the crash. But I'm fine now. Honestly."

I knew she was lying to herself. She might've been right about not actually *seeing* anything, but she knew she wasn't alone out there. She knew she was being hunted and it was her primal flight response that possibly saved her life.

"But forget all of that," she said. "Why are we back in the van? And where's Wyatt?"

Sahrye grabbed Clare's good hand firmly and said, "Aaron said there was something running around out there. A bear or a wolf or something. We think it might've…"

Sahrye trailed off when Clare pulled back her hand and stared at her suspiciously. "Might've what? So something IS out there? Wyatt is still out there and you both just left him?!"

"Keep your voice down," I snapped. "It might still be out there."

"What?" Clare asked. Her voice trembled as it filled with frustration.

"Yeah, Aaron," Sahrye added. "You never told me what you saw."

I looked at both of the women and sighed, knowing I had to attempt to tell them, whether they'd believe me or not.

"It was…big. Almost like a tall person but it was hunched on all fours. It had fur but I swear it had bone and flesh poking through it. And it had a weird face. I couldn't believe it at first but it was like a big deer skull, with antlers. And I saw it…It attacked Wyatt."

Both women stared at me in silence. It was awkward to say the least but the longer we sat the more I realized they didn't believe a single word.

"You've got to be shitting me," Clare responded. She turned to Sahrye and said,"So this is what I have to go through? You and your boyfriend play make believe with some creepy pasta bullshit while my fiancé is still out there alone?"

Sahrye sat in silence, not sure if she wanted to even comment about what I just said.

"But it's the truth," I said, "I-I don't know what it is and I don't want to go into details about what I saw. It was horrible and disgusting and—"

I stopped when I saw Clare rush for her luggage and use her good hand to dig inside. She pulled out a flashlight and began to make her way back to the van's door. I immediately moved over to block her.

"Aaron, what the fuck is wrong with you?" she cried angrily.

"You can't go back out there. It's not safe. That thing might still be there."

Clare continued to squeeze by me. "Aaron, I was literally just out there. There's nothing out there. We're all just suffering through trauma or something. We'll figure this shit out in the morning but now I need to find Wyatt. He's my future husband!"

I knew talking to her was no use so I had no choice. I pulled the revolver from my coat pocket and pointed it at Clare. Both her and Sahrye gasped.

Sahrye held up her hands and yelled, "Babe stop! What are you doing? Don't shoot her! Are you insane?"

"I said you can't go out there. I know what I saw. That thing will kill you. It will kill ALL of us. We have to wait until morning. You two have to trust me on this."

Clare stared back at me defiantly and pushed herself in front of me, standing an inch away from the revolver. "If you're gonna shoot, then shoot. But I'm going out there."

I looked into her eyes. She was serious. I decided that firing the gun was too messy and too loud for this situation. Hesitantly, I placed it back in my coat pocket and scooted away from the door. Clare brushed past me and began to pull the handle and slide the door.

Sahrye and I watched as she opened the door and turned on her flashlight. Just as she was about to step out, however, she looked down on the ground and froze. She let out the loudest, blood-curdling shriek I've ever heard. She covered her face and cried as she turned away from the door and jumped into the back of the van.

Me and Sahrye turned to Clare, who was now curled up in the backseat and whimpering as she shivered in terror. We both slowly crept to the door and looked down where she had looked. We both nearly choked on our vomit.

In the snow was a pile of flesh and blood. A small mound of crushed bones, entrails and other remains sat below. There was a red trail leading from the pitch-blackness of the woods, as if something dragged the flesh directly to us. Blood still dripped from the bones and the intestines, giving us the indication that it was fresh. Beside the bloody mess sat Wyatt's cell phone with the shattered screen, and it somehow looked more damaged than it did before.

I immediately rushed to slam the van door shut and locked it. Me and Sahrye then pushed ourselves to the opposite side of the van, far away from the door where the pile of gore stood.

We stayed awake for the rest of the night. Not only were we disturbed knowing that our friend was most likely reduced to a blob of torn flesh, but also by the fact that whatever the creature was that did this was still out there. Worst of all, it knew where we were.

I was the first to slowly open the van door the following morning. I don't know how to explain it, but I figured after everything the ladies had to deal with the day before, it would be better if I took the first peek outside. The morning birds chirping and the warm glow from the sunrise gave the impression that the long night was over. Of course, I knew better than to assume we were safe just because the sun was out.

I slowly pushed the door open and peeked out. I could feel the gradual heating of the air from the outside due to the sunrise. The snow that the storm left yesterday was almost reduced to puddles and soft slush. Even the frost and ice that coated the van earlier had completely melted.

It would be a decent scenery to enjoy, if it wasn't for the gruesome mess still sitting in front of the door. The blob of flesh and bones was still there. The smell was horrid. I had to use my shirt to cover my face to keep from throwing up. It had been almost a full day since the last time I'd eaten anything, and I didn't want whatever I had left in my system to be wasted on the ground.

I looked back at the girls who waited for me to see if outside was safe. I nodded to them and held out my hand toward Sahrye. She was hesitant at first when she saw I had my shirt covering half of my face. She slowly grabbed my hand and followed me out of the van. She took a mournful and pitiful glance at the bodily remains on the ground and she too pulled her shirt over her nose.

It took a while for us to convince Clare to leave the van, especially knowing that she'd have to walk over whatever remained of her decimated fiancé. To say I felt bad was an understatement. I felt guilty and disgusted about the whole thing, but we couldn't stay in the forest. Even Clare understood that the place was too dangerous to spend another second in.

We finally had sunlight to help us get up the hill. I asked Clare if her arm was doing okay. She gave a weak nod, even though I knew it was probably still in pain after she tampered with it last night. It seemed to have stopped bleeding, although the dressing was dark brown after soaking in blood all night.

The three of us took our time maneuvering up the hill. We took as many bags as we could carry on our own, leaving behind the ones that we couldn't. The trees, bushes and boulders didn't make it an easy hike, but me and Sahrye managed to keep our footing while occasionally keeping an eye on Clare. There were a couple of times when we had to take turns helping her over a rocky ledge on our way up. Despite the struggle and sun that was starting to beam heavily on my back, it brought me a light sense of relief when I saw the van slowly disappear from view. I tried to not give it too much attention, but from my last couple of glances back, it almost looked like the flesh was no longer there. I couldn't tell if that was due to the distance or my imagination, but I could hardly see the remains anymore, almost as if it vanished after we left. Or rather, something took it away.

It felt like an hour had passed when we reached the top of the hill. That was when we saw it: the highway. We could see the deep tire marks in the dirt from where our van was knocked off of the road and down the hill. On the other side of the road was another set of tire marks, possibly made by the car that hit us. Whatever type of vehicle it was, it must've just sped away after the collision. Lucky for them I guess.

Sahrye had the idea to hitchhike down the road from where we originally came, at least until we were able to find a passerby kind enough to give us a lift to the nearest town. Otherwise, we would just walk until we found a sign pointing back to the interstate. Sahrye reminded me that we needed to find a hospital ASAP so Clare could get better medical attention. Clare protested that she was fine and that the bleeding had stopped, but Sahrye wasn't hearing any of it.

We walked for a few miles. We shared a water bottle along the way to keep hydrated and we passed around a bag of Doritos, gummy worms and a Hershey bar for nourishment. It wasn't healthy or filling, but it would have to do.

After a while, our feet began to get sore and we became more fatigued than we could bear. Sahrye turned to me while taking deep, heavy breaths. Beads of sweat covered her forehead, causing her raven hair to stick as if she had dipped her head in a sink full of water. "I think...we should take a break."

"Agreed," Clare called, leaning against a tree while clutching her arm. I was also drained and sleep deprived, but I wasn't ready to sit down yet. Although we'd made it to the highway, we were still in the middle of nowhere. To make matters worse, we'd been walking for the majority of the morning and still hadn't seen another car yet.

Just as my last thought passed, I stopped mid-step when I heard a sound from behind us. It sounded like the hum of an engine. All three of us looked at each other to see if we all heard the same thing. We turned and to our surprise, a green, partially rusted pickup truck was slowly cruising down the road from behind us.

Immediately we all waved the truck down and yelled, desperately trying to get the driver's attention. Luckily, the truck slowed to a gentle halt on the side of the road. The three of us limped over to the vehicle, trying our best to regain our composure and not come off as a bunch of hobos or prison escapees.

As we got close, the driver's window rolled down quickly. A tanned, older man with sand-colored hair poked his head out..

"Are you people alright?" he asked us with sincere concern. His voice was gruff, almost matching his weathered face that suggested his age to be somewhere in his late fifties to mid-sixties. From the open window, I could smell the hint of cigarettes.

Sahrye was the first to respond. She approached his window and tried her best to sound as convincingly helpless as possible.

"Excuse me, sir," she started calmly. "We had an accident and our car slipped off the road. Only one of us has a phone, but it's dead, so we couldn't call anyone. We were wondering if you knew where the nearest town was so we could help our friend out." She gestured toward Clare, who stood beside me with her stained arm wrapping.

The man's eyes glossed over the three of us as he was deciding if he could buy Sahrye's story. He then asked, "Which way were you all heading?"

"North. For the Montana state line," she added.

The man shook his head and spoke with a sympathetic tone. "I'm afraid you folks chose the worst place to have an accident. The nearest town is east of here, and that ain't for another ninety miles. Let's just say well over an hour drive, which is even longer on foot. And their hospital is even farther out than that."

The three of us looked at each other with the utmost disappointment. There was no way we were continuing that journey on foot in our condition. I looked back at Sahrye, hoping she would say something to the stranger to convince him to actually help instead of just giving vague directions.

Sahrye turned back to the man and said, "Thanks for telling us that but we were hoping that you could give us a lift. Just get us as close as you can. The hospital you mentioned would be great but even if you can't, we can pay you. We have money."

"How much?" the man quickly asked with a raised eyebrow. I did the quick mental math and remembered that I still had just over three hundred dollars in cash on me. I usually brought that amount on our trips in case of emergencies.

I spoke up and said, "One fifty to get us to the hospital." I held up a few bills in my hand to show my sincerity. The man looked at the cash and thought about it.

"Young man," he said, chuckling, "I was gonna help anyway. I wasn't expecting cash, but since you're offering I'm gonna hold you to it. Now here's the thing. I was actually heading home to do some work on my roof today. Been putting it off for a while now, but anyway, the house is only two miles down this road. My wife, Olivia, used to be a nurse in the Army Medical Department. She's been retired for a few years, but I bet your hundred and fifty bucks that she'll take faster care of that arm than that town will. We can still drop you off there after you all get properly patched up."

We looked at each other and for the first time since the crash we realized that we were covered in scars and bruises. The dirt almost concealed most of them but we were so focused on Clare's arm that we didn't notice. The idea sounded both convenient and sketchy at the same time. The man was a complete stranger, despite him being somewhat cordial. Something about getting "patched up" at a stranger's home in the woods just didn't sit too well with me. On the other hand, I realized that Clare looked a little paler than she had this morning. She had bags under her eyes and she was almost hunched over from trying to hold the bloodied wrapping over her arm. I could tell Sahrye felt horrible about the pain her friend was going through. Hell, so did I. The longer we waited, the worse the wound could become.

We reluctantly agreed on the man's offer and allowed ourselves into his pickup. I went to the front seat while the ladies sat in the back. We placed our bags on the bed of the truck next to a couple of large paint cans, some hammers, and an extendable ladder.

The man introduced himself as Roy, and he had been living in Wyoming for his entire life moving from job to job. He bragged about his affinity for manual labor or tasks that required a decent amount of strength, will, and a desire to get your hands dirty. I figured he was looking to just have a conversation to last for the ride, so we continued to converse along the way to get better acquainted. When he eventually asked about the accident, I managed to interject before Sahrye or Clare could answer.

I mentioned the snow-storm, the slick road, and our original planned trip to Montana. I deliberately altered some details, thinking it was best to not mention too much information for him to draw his own conclusions. Afterall, I still didn't exactly trust him enough to tell the whole story. Instead of telling him about the van being rear-ended and pushed down a hill, I told him our car slid and crashed into a tree. I figured if he spread that story, then perhaps people wouldn't be in a hurry to find a van crashed in the woods with human body parts being dragged around it.

Fortunately, he didn't ask too many questions about the crash, so I didn't have to tell any more lies. All that mattered now was finding help for Clare's arm and a way to get back to town to find a way home. I'd worry about the van's insurance, Wyatt's family, and a dozen other fucked-up problems later.

Of course, during the ride, I made sure to never mention the skull-faced animal I saw in the woods the previous night. I knew he would probably assume I was nuts and would end up having second thoughts about helping us. Instead I kept that detail to myself and carried on with the small talk until we pulled onto a dirt pathway. The path stretched up a small hill where the man's house stood.

The house was what you would expect an old couple living in the woods to reside in: an average-sized cabin with a small dirt lot around it. A few chickens walked around and pecked at the ground. As we got out of the truck, they all scattered out of our way. Roy led the way to his front door and

I followed close behind. I noticed Sahrye and Clare slightly trailing behind, glancing at the surroundings. The woods around the home were just as dense and tall as the woods where we spent the night. The only difference now was that we knew that there were people living there, so we weren't exactly alone. But that only brought a minimal amount of comfort.

A silver-haired woman appeared from behind an opening screen door. She looked middle-aged and wore a tank-top with a flower-printed robe, along with loose-fitting jeans. Her style of clothing almost reminded me of what the hippies would wear in the 70s. When she first stepped onto the porch, she took a glance at us. The look she had was confused and somewhat judgmental, but it immediately morphed into a kind smile as her husband got close enough to give her a kiss on the cheek.

"My oh my, what a surprise," chimed Roy's wife, Olivia. "If only Roy would've warned me about guests coming over, I would've been better pre- pared." Roy coughed and chuckled nervously to recover from the indirect scolding by his wife.

He then smiled and wrapped one arm around her shoulder as he turned towards us. "Olivia, let me get you acquainted with these kind youngsters I've had the pleasure of meeting today. The lad over there is Aaron. The sweet doll right there is Sara."

Sahrye quickly raised her hand and politely interjected. "It's Sahrye, sir."

Roy placed his palm on his forehead and chuckled. "Sahrye. That's right. My bad, darling." He then pointed to Clare, who stood sheepishly behind Sahrye. "And that poor soul over there is Miss Clare. They had a bit of an accident from the snowstorm yesterday, and she got the brunt of the whole thing as you can see."

Roy gestured to Clare's bloodied bandage and the arm that barely hung in it. Olivia took a long and pitiful glance at the arm and placed her hand over her chest, as if the sight of the injury was hard for her to look at.

"Oh dear," she exclaimed,"That looks a lot more than a broken arm. You must've been cut, sweetie. It doesn't even look like it's been given a proper cleaning, let alone any ointment."

Sahrye said,"Roy said the nearest town was over an hour away, and that the hospital was even farther than that. He said you have experience with medical emergencies, so we figured if you can help us, we could pay you for the troubles and we'll be on our way."

"Oh, there ain't no trouble here, sweetheart," said Olivia in a soothing, motherly tone. "And yes, I used to be a nurse in the Army for over twenty years, and I've experienced plenty of cuts and broken limbs before. Just come inside and let's get you all cleaned up. And for God's sake, let's get rid of the awful wrapping on your arm."

I wasn't sure how Clare felt after hearing that, since the bloodied wrapping was pretty much the last thing Wyatt had given her before he was killed, despite its poor usefulness.

Just as promised, Olivia and Roy led us inside their home and directed me and Sahrye to the bathroom, while Olivia took Clare to the kitchen sink. We weren't in the kitchen when Olivia was changing Clare's bandage to clean and examine her injury, but we still heard her wince and yelp as Olivia whispered to her in a soothing tone. As for me and Sahrye, we only took a quick shower together to get rid of the dirt and sweat. There were a few scratches here and there on our faces, arms and legs, but we just used some Neosporin and band-aids that Roy handed to us.

After we dried off and put on some spare clothes that Roy had offered us, we left the bathroom and made our way through the cabin. Though it was small, the couple managed to make it look spacious from the inside. We saw a few hanging photos of the couple at what seemed to be family gatherings and trips. We saw one in which Roy was hugging Olivia romantically from behind. They were both smiling as they stood in front of what looked like the stone structures of Machu Picchu in Peru. I looked at the photo and wondered if me and Sahrye would ever be a traveling, adventurous couple again after everything that had happened.

We made a turn from one of the halls into the living room where other frames sat. Most of these looked like painted art-work rather than photos. Roy walked past us on his way to check on his wife and Clare in the kitchen. "Oh, and feel free to check out Olivia's artwork. Other than nursing, she's a damn good painter."

When he walked off, Sahrye tapped on my shoulder and laughed at one painting of a woman who was painting a portrait of herself. "Look close. You can almost tell that that's supposed to be Olivia in both paintings. It's like she was painting a self-portrait creating another self-portrait. That's amazing, isn't it?"

She turned to me as I stood with my jaw dropped. She was confused at first until she followed my eyes and found that I wasn't staring at the same painting as she was. In front of me was a different painting, one with darker colors and a morbid feeling coming from it.

It was a painting of a rocky landscape with dark clouds and a navy-blue haze. In the center of the picture was a creature with gray, sickly skin with fur patches scattered across its back and neck. Its stance was bipedal like a human, but there was nothing human about it at all. It stood on its hind legs, which looked bent and crooked, as if they belonged to a crossbreed of a horse and a werewolf. Its feet were large hooves that dwarfed those of a moose or cow. Its body was arched and a hump protruded from its back. The arms were so abnormally long that the creature's pitch-black raptor claws nearly dragged on the ground. Out of all the strange and gruesome features the creature had, the most unsettling was the head: an elongated skull of a deer. The mouth of the beast was gaped wide open in an eternal roar.

"That's it," I choked. Sahrye scrunched her brows as she looked at the illustration of the same monster I saw the night before. The same abomination that pounced on Wyatt and ripped him to pieces and left his remains next to our van to spite us.

"What are you saying?"Sahrye asked.

"That," I whispered pointing at the artwork, "was what I saw last night. That's what killed Wyatt."

Sahrye looked back and forth between me and the picture with concern. "Aaron. Please. We don't know what happened. It was probably a bear or a wolf or something big."

"What wolf or bear have you seen that looks like that?" I snapped. Sahrye took a step back in shock but I no longer cared. I knew what I saw and I knew it couldn't just be a coincidence that the same creature was in the picture. There was a chance that the couple knew it, and had maybe even seen it themselves.

Roy returned from the kitchen and shot a suspicious and concerned look at us. "Everything alright over here?"

Me and Sahrye turned, startled. I was still distracted by my haunting memory of the monster and my frustration at Sahrye for not believing me, even after what we saw next to the van.

"Oh, we're fine," Sahrye said, breaking the uncomfortable silence. "We were just checking out your wife's work."

Roy nodded and his face returned to its relaxed state. His eyes then glazed past us toward the illustration of the monster.

"Ah, I remember that one," he said with a reminiscent smile. "She painted that years ago, shortly after we got married. She called it 'The Wendigo'. She told me that it was based on an old tale that her family used to pass down for generations. She's part Cree, you see."

Wendigo, my mind repeated. I tried to recall where and when I'd heard that word before.

"What exactly is a Wendigo?" I asked. "Is it an animal or something?"

Roy shrugged and said, "Beats me. I think it's one of those scary tales used to convince children from wandering around the woods alone. But I don't know the whole lore. You're gonna have to ask Olivia about that. Lucky for you, she just got done fixing your friend in there and she's about to get started on lunch. I don't drive on an empty stomach, so I'm gonna stick around and get a bite. You should join us. Maybe she'll tell you the story about the Wendigo better than I could."

I thought about the idea and realized that it was a little past noon. I felt that we were spending too much time on this fucked-up trip. But before I could respond, Sahrye interjected and said with a wide smile, "That actually sounds great. We actually came up this way to explore for a while. Yeah, we got derailed, but it wouldn't hurt to make the best of what we got, right?"

Roy smiled in approval of Sahrye's optimism, although it was really her way to end the conversation between me and him. Roy went into a closet and pulled out a large extendable ladder. He then continued his way toward the front screen door and said, "Welp, I gotta get started on that roof. I'm gonna take a look at it for now to decide on the shingle work it needs. I should be back down in a half-hour or whenever lunch is ready. If you need anything, just holler at Olivia." With that, he took the ladder over his shoulder and headed out the door.

Sahrye waved at Roy as the door closed behind him. We both looked at each other for a brief moment. She switched to a serious demeanor and narrowed her eyes up at me. This was her way of telling me to drop our recent dispute, although I already realized it was pointless to bring up the matter.

We made our way into the kitchen to see Clare sitting on a wooden stool and Olivia washing her hands in the sink. I saw a pair of vinyl gloves covered in blood sitting on the side of the sink and a couple of balled-up sheets of gauze soaked with blood as well. Clare raised her head at me and Sahrye and gave a delicate smile. The pain from getting her arm treated must've been so intense and agonizing that even smiling was a strain.

"Hey, guys," she said while waving her good hand. Her other arm was wrapped, although this time the wrapping was white and unsullied. On the counter-top, next to the gauze, was a bloodied needle and a jumbled strand of thread. Sahrye's eyes dropped from the threads and to Clare's arm.

"Clare," she started almost breathlessly, "what happened?"

Clare looked down at her bandaged arm and shrugged. "Well, I got fixed. Still hurts like hell, but it actually feels better than before."

That was when Olivia began scooping up the bloodied gauze and old bandage. "I bet it does," she said. She then turned to the garbage beside the counter and tossed the old material into the trash. After doing so, she turned to us with her arms crossed. "Your friend here was lucky to find us. Whoever wrapped it previously did manage to make a decent splint after pushing the bones back in place, but she had an open wound underneath it. It didn't look like it's been given any attention at all."

Clare shrugged. "I didn't notice it before. It got wrapped up right after the crash. The scar probably opened overnight."

"Yeah," I added. "Plus, we didn't really have any medical supplies with us at the time. It was getting too dark to leave from where we were, so we ended up spending the night there."

"In the woods?" Olivia said with a shocked expression. "That must've been one hell of a night. I'm glad to see all of you survived."

The three of us looked at each other, knowing that was far from the truth. We all understood that just as Wyatt had died, we could've easily died along with him.

About an hour later, Olivia called for us to join her at the table in the living room. We all sat around it as she came towards the table with a large metal pot she held with oven mitts around the handles. She placed the pot at the center of the table. She then passed each of us an empty bowl with a spoon wrapped neatly in a napkin in the manner the waiters at a fancy restaurant present their silverware to their guests. She then took the top of the pot off, releasing a puff of steam to bloom into the air like a small mushroom cloud. We peered into the pot and saw that it was a stew filled with bits of corn, specks of green herbs, small black beans, and chunks of squash. The spicy and hearty aroma made my mouth water. The smell was immaculate, but the nutty and savory taste was even more so.

I had at least two bowls of the stew, almost forgetting I was merely a guest being treated by complete strangers. At first we felt almost like a burden, or invaders even, for entering the couple's home, using their shower, and now eating their food. But there we were, chatting, joking, and enjoying each other's company. If it weren't for Clare's arm being wrapped up, we probably could have forgotten about the past misfortunes.

My memories came flooding back when I caught a glimpse of the dark painting of the Wendigo. I almost struggled swallowing the chunk of squash I was chewing on when I remembered the horror I'd witnessed and struggled to get my girlfriend or Clare to understand. I knew if I asked Olivia what I wanted to ask her, Sahrye and Clare would probably never forgive me. Unfortunately, the question escaped my lips before I could stop myself.

"Excuse me, ma'am," I said after swallowing a mouthful of stew, "I noticed your artwork and I just had to ask you something."

Sahrye was already staring at me, her eyes pierced me like daggers. *Here goes nothing*, I thought. I nodded at the Wendigo painting and asked, "What inspired you to do *that* painting?"

Olivia turned and looked at the painting I was referring to: the Wendigo standing in bipedal position, its jaws gaping wide open while seemingly staring back at her. "Oh, that?" she asked as she repositioned herself to face me. "That's called the Wendigo, or Witiko, depending who you ask. When I was a child, I grew up on an old reservation in Alberta. The elders of the town, especially my grandparents, used to tell us stories about Witiko. They would sit all of the children down and tell us about a man who was from an ancient tribe in a much more ancient land who had upset nature by disobeying one of its oldest laws: to never eat flesh from another human."

I sat and listened intently as Olivia spoke and noticed that she was no longer eating the stew. Even Sahrye and Clare stopped eating to listen to her, almost sitting at the edge of their seats. Olivia was staring down at her bowl while she twirled her spoon around the edge of it. It was as if she was accessing an old memory that she had kept buried in the back of her mind for a long time.

"There are many versions of how the first Witiko came into being," she continued. "But each of them mentions something about cannibalism. Now, mind you, many creatures tend to cannibalize each other when food is scarce, but it has been believed that nature holds humans to a higher standard, so there are laws that are set in place that, despite how superior we think we are, even we are compelled to obey. Cannibalism is regarded as an unforgivable sin, so when a person devours the flesh of another, they get punished."

The room was quiet for a moment. Me and the girls were all curious now. "Um, punished?" I asked.

"Yes," Olivia said in a matter-of-fact tone. "The story tells of a cannibalistic tribal member who devoured another member of his tribe. Afterward, nature punished him by putting him through a terrible transformation. His body twisted into an animalistic yet unnatural shape. He grew antlers, hooves, fangs, claws, fur, and even some of his skin began to tear away because the transformation was so intense and brutal. But other than describing how ugly the cannibal became, another thing that all the stories had in common was the Witiko's insatiable hunger. Just like his immortal life, his hunger for human flesh is also eternal. No matter how much he eats, he desires more."

I took in every word of the story. The details, such as the fur, the fangs and the antlers, all matched with what I saw the previous night and what the painting presented. I wondered how she was able to depict the creature with such accuracy. Even the color of the fur, the length of the claws, and the shape of the head of the monster almost matched the exact same beast I'd seen.

I was about to question her on her accuracy with the artwork and if she has seen the Wendigo, or Witiko, or whatever. Suddenly, Clare said, "And *that* was supposed to be a story for kids?"

Before Olivia could respond, the front door opened and closed. Roy came in with his ladder over his shoulder and began to push it back into the closet. Olivia called to him and said, "The stew is ready, Roy. I added extra garlic this time. Should help with all this bipolar weather we've been getting. I know you're not trying to get sick."

"Thank you, Ollie. Speaking of weather, I've been listening to the radio while I was checking on the roof. They said another snowstorm is coming within the hour."

"Should we leave now then?" Clare asked, "We can outrun it, can't we?"

"Oh no. I don't think so, young lady. I know y'all from out of town but the snow here makes the roads very difficult to navigate. And the clouds are already coming over us, which is a bummer for me because there ain't no way I can do anything to that roof now."

"So what does that mean for us?" I asked. "Is there somewhere closer we can go for the night?"

Roy shook his head and threw up his hands. "I've lived around these parts for a good portion of my life, bud. If there was a motel around here, I would drive you all there ASAP. But getting you all to that town is just too risky. The radio said they're expecting 45 mph winds and six feet of snow, and unlike yesterday, this snow ain't gonna be gone by the morning. Now, we do have a spare room we keep for relatives, and we got a couch down here. If you'd all like to stay the extra night, you can."

"What? No, we can't," I said. "I mean, you two did so much already."

Olivia interrupted as she reached and placed a hand on my shoulder and said, "Aaron, you're not bothering us. That room hasn't been slept in since last summer when we had a family gathering. It's plenty of room for you and Sahrye."

"Yeah, and I don't really mind sleeping on the couch anyway," Clare exclaimed. I shot her a stare and thought, *Seriously?*

Before I could argue against staying for another night, Sahrye decided to join in. "I think that'll be fine. In fact, I don't mind helping out around the house if you need us to."

Roy smiled and said, "I'm gonna hold you to that. And besides, we're good Christian folk. We don't get too many visitors out here, so when we find a chance to bring some kindness into the world, we take it."

I realized there was no point in arguing with these people, so I just went along with it. As we all finished eating, I looked out the window and shuddered when I saw thick white flurries falling on the ground. The rest of the afternoon was spent helping the couple around the house. We swept their attic, mopped the kitchen floor tiles, and helped usher their chickens into the coop before the snowfall increased. Roy asked me to help him move some tools and farm gear into his shed out back. As we did, I noticed that there were tall garden torches with glass shields over the tops that stood in the lawn. None of them were lit, but there were over a dozen of them and they circled the perimeter of the home.

Roy noticed me staring at the torch stands and said,"Oh, Olivia made me install those when we got this house years ago. She goes out here every now and then to light all of them before sunset. It's a traditional thing she and her people used to do. I thought it was a weird idea at first, but when you live with someone long enough, you tend to overlook all the quirky things they do."

"I never saw this many torches in one place," I said. "It's like a setup for a pagan ritual or something."

Roy shrugged. "Yeah. Believe me, as a Christian man I thought this was beyond odd. Hell, I figured she was gonna make a blood sacrifice or something. Her family is Christian too, but they still carry on some traditions that their ancestors did. It took a while, but I eventually got used to some of the weird things she does."

I nodded in understanding and we both walked through the rising snow as we returned to the cabin. We spent a few hours watching TV and conversing and had dinner. After we washed our dishes, I looked out the window above the sink and noticed someone was walking around out there in a large thick coat. The bottom of their pants were swallowed up by the snow that accumulated on the ground. From the looks of it, the snow was still coming down, but the figure seemed unfazed by it. I looked closer to get a better look at their face. It was Olivia. She carried a box of matches and walked up to one of the torches. She lit a match and slowly opened the glass covering and lit it, allowing a ball of flame to grow inside the case. She did the same thing for all the torches until the entire property was surrounded. *Strange. Very strange,* I thought to myself. I eventually returned my attention to my dishes to avoid making awkward eye contact with Olivia.

Afterward, we all prepared for bed. As me and Sahrye went to the spare bedroom, she decided to confront me about the discussion between me and Olivia earlier.

"Aaron, I think we need to talk," she said after taking a deep breath.

"About?" I asked.

"What happened earlier? Remember that Wendigo picture thing? Well, the discussion you and Olivia had was bothering Clare."

"Bothering her?"

"Yeah. She said it was bothering her ever since she told us about her running in the woods from her 'imagination,' and then you told us about the thing you saw."

"And you still don't believe me. Yes, I know. Why are you two worried about it now?"

"I'm not, but you're the one who said that the monster from some Native American myth killed Wyatt. And then you and Olivia were talking about it. That's not helping. Clare needs to heal, not hear about some deer monster that killed her fiancé last night."

"But it did, Sahrye! Why won't you believe me? You saw his body too. I know you did. You know there wasn't a normal animal that could do that and leave it in front of the van."

I realized I was yelling now and tried to regain my composure. Sahrye shook her head and said, "I don't know anything, Aaron. I don't know what you saw. And I'm not saying you didn't see anything. But what I'm saying is that yesterday was very traumatic for all of us. Clare said she imagined she heard something following her. She was wounded and had a broken arm. Who knows what was going on in her head. And maybe you did see an animal out there, but you were so traumatized from the crash that you probably imagined bizarre details that just simply weren't there. I mean, you literally hit your head when we crashed. I had to pull you out of the van myself. I know you couldn't have been well."

At first I was livid at the fact that my own girlfriend was basically calling me insane and saying that my brain was so broken that I was just imagining everything. Then I thought back again to the picture and the accuracy of it and began to wonder.

"Hey," I said, partially thinking out loud, "hear me out, but what if this is all part of a set-up?"

"What?"

"Listen. The picture of the monster is exactly how it looked last night. That can't be coincidental."

"Aaron…"

"Maybe there isn't a Wendigo. Maybe the creature was really them the whole time. Like a costume or something."

"You can't be serious." Sahrye turned away and changed her clothes and began to climb into the bed.

"No. Listen," I persisted. "What if these guys are serial killers or something? Think about it. They're too nice and comfortable with us. They live in the middle of the woods, and Roy pulled up almost as soon as we left the crash site."

I was going to tell Sahrye about when I saw Olivia lighting up torches in the middle of a snowstorm when she placed her head on the pillow, her back turned toward me. "These are good people, Aaron. And if you're so suspicious to call them murderers after all the nice things they've done for us, then you're welcome to go to town by yourself. Just try to stay on the road if you can."

I said nothing. Not because I didn't want to. Believe me, I had plenty more I wanted to say but I didn't. It was pointless trying to argue with her at this point. I wasn't lying about my suspicions of the couple. I went to one side of the room where a wooden chair stood. I picked it up, walked towards the door and propped the chair under the door handle at an angle that would make it difficult for anyone to sneak into the room. I then crawled into bed next to Sahrye and turned facing the window. My coat I wore earlier lay on the floor below me. I made sure to place it so that the revolver I left in the pocket was only an arm's reach away.

Call me paranoid. Hell, call me insane. Everyone else had, but I just didn't care. Too much had happened in so little time. If these people did have an alternative motive, I won't make it easy for them.

My eyes flickered open. The room was almost pitch-black now, except for the LCD lights that showed the time on the alarm clock on the dresser next to the bed. It was a quarter to one in the morning.

I sat up in bed and looked at the window. The blinds were thick and shut, but I could see through the very thin slits between them that the torches outside were still glowing. I then turned to the door to see what had woken me up so early. The chair was still propped under the doorknob where I left it. I looked down to see Sahrye was still sound asleep. Her mouth gaped open as she snored and drooled onto her pillow. *Damn shame that Olivia is gonna have to clean that*, I thought.

I was about to lie back down to return to sleep when something caught my attention. It was the sound of something clattering. I sat up slowly, trying to determine what could make that sound and where it was coming from. I slowed my breathing and listened. Then it happened again. It was something quick, small, yet it reverberated with a metallic ting. It was also just on the other side of the door.

I slowly pulled myself out of bed, put on a pair of pants, socks, boots, and my coat that was on the floor. All the while, I kept listening to the metallic sound that rhythmically continued. I made my way to the door and quietly moved the chair aside. I slowly opened the door, trying to keep it from creaking. I looked beyond and peered down a dark hallway. It was hard to see much of anything without a reliable source of light, but from the light from the windows, I was able to see outlines of some objects in the hall. Suddenly, I heard the sound again, this time it was right in front of me. I looked down only to find that the sound came from a metal bucket placed at the front of the doorway. There was about a quarter-inch of water in it, revealing only an outline of my reflection. I looked up just in time to see a water droplet fall from the ceiling into the bucket, turning my reflection into a series of ripples.

What the hell is wrong with me? I thought to myself, feeling like a complete idiot for peeking out of the room just to discover that I'd been startled by a bucket of water. The roof must've had so much snow on it that it was starting to leak, and since Roy wasn't able to climb up and fix it, he must've placed buckets all over the house. Speaking of which, I could hear a loud, deep snore coming from the bedroom at the other end of the hall. Somehow I knew it was Roy and I didn't feel the need to investigate to be sure.

After getting my coat, I decided to close the door and head downstairs to the living room to check on Clare, who claimed the couch for herself. If what Sahrye said was true and I did upset her by asking about the Wendigo, then I guess I could try to apologize. Or at least try to figure out if she was doing okay after everything that happened. When I got to the living room, however, the couch was empty. I noticed a blanket was pushed aside, as if someone was recently laying down and got up with haste.

I suddenly felt uncomfortable. This part of the house was not only silent, but also dark, except for a few glowing electronic clocks. Other than that, there was this large glow from the front of the room. I realized it was the same light I saw from the spare bedroom from the torches outside. I walked past the couch and my heart jumped in surprise. The front door was wide open.

I couldn't understand who would just open it in the middle of the night. Snow flurries floated in from outside as I walked closer to it. Luckily I already had my boots on, because the thick pile of snow on the porch was starting to melt and seep into the doorway due to the warmth of the house.

I found myself walking closer outside the doorway and I looked beyond the porch where I stood. The tribal torches were still lit, their fires blazing and dancing in the glass containers that protected them from the oncoming snow. I decided to stand out there and look around for a minute. I just wanted to know who would run out and leave the door wide open at this hour.

I peered into the woods beyond the flaming torches. They now looked just as dark and thick as the woods we were running in before, only now there was more light between me and the tall, shadowy, menacing trees that towered over the property. I was about to give up and return to the house when my eyes caught movement. There was something that bobbed up and down behind the bushes. I squinted my eyes to get a better look, knowing that whatever it was, it had to still be behind the bushes. I felt the urge to call out just to let whoever or whatever it was know that I was aware of its presence. I didn't need to.

The bush rustled as something bulky and hairy stretched past it. Then another shape stretched out and twitched as it felt the ground. I thought to myself, *They look like…like hands. No. Claws!* Sure enough, the shapes turned out to be large, dark claws covered in patches of fur and veins.

The pitch-black curved nails almost scraped against the ground as they moved and pushed themselves up for the rest of the body to stand upright. There was a silhouette of a tall, humanoid shape that hunched forward as it walked on two hind legs that resembled those of an elk trying to do a poor and clumsy impression of a human walking. The legs bent at an angle that reminded me of the werewolf from the *Harry Potter* movie I watched when I was a kid, only they looked bony and sickly.

The rest of the creature continued to move closer to the torch's light, revealing the rest of its body, forcing me to freeze in absolute terror. The hulking being hunched forward with its abnormally large arms hung close to the ground. Sinew could be seen as if pieces of flesh had been ripped off long ago, but instead of healing, the wounds festered and grew over themselves. Its chest and abdomen were similar to a large human's except covered in patches of fur and rotting wounds, some revealing ribs and moldy flesh. Its head was facing my direction, a massive skull that looked like it once belonged to a long-deceased moose or deer and was forcibly placed onto the shoulders of this abomination. The skull was the color of ivory with a tint of brown on its lower sides. Its antlers were large enough to knock down the tree branches if the creature had a straighter posture. Wisps of steam came from the nasal cavity of the skull and the mouth.

I stood in disbelief and horror at what I was looking at, but I somehow knew that this was the same beast that I saw butcher and devour my friend only one night ago. This was the Wendigo, and he had followed us.

The Wendigo's chest and shoulders heaved as his empty eye sockets aimed at me. It was a strange and nerve-wracking feeling to be stared at by something that didn't have eyes, but was somehow looking directly into your soul. The beast took a large, heavy step forward, crushing the ice and snow beneath his massive hooves. Immediately, I reached into my pocket and aimed the revolver at the monster. He looked at the gun and tilted his head to the side like a curious dog looking at a brand new chew-toy. Then he turned his head to his original position and made a deep, hefty, guttural sound that made my heart race. He was laughing at me.

I knew I had to act. I didn't want to end up like Wyatt, and I damn sure didn't want it anywhere near Sahrye or the others. Part of me hoped that this was a costume, but at this point my primal instincts demanded that I defend myself. I flicked the handle back on the gun and aimed at the creature. My hand shook as I tried to focus. Then someone behind me spoke and caught my attention.

"That'll be a waste of bullets," the voice behind me said calmly. I turned my head in shock, my heart nearly ready to leap from my throat. It was Olivia.

"O-Olivia? What–"

Olivia was standing in the center of the doorway. *Was she the one who opened the door*? I wondered. I thought about it and realized that she must've followed me from *inside* the house. "Witiko isn't afraid of bullets. It'll piss him off, but that won't really slow him down if he was gonna kill you."

I was confused but I immediately returned my gaze to the Wendigo, who was staring at me and now Olivia too.

"Th-That's the, um," I stammered.

"Witiko," Olivia corrected me. "And yes the legend is true. At least for him it is."

"What is he doing? Is he here to kill us?"

Olivia chuckled, as if to mock the monster that stared at us. I saw his shoulders rise and drop heavily as he grew agitated. "Oh, trust me, he wants to. More than anything. But you don't have to worry."

"Are you serious? He's looking directly at me. You said bullets won't do anything?"

Olivia shrugged and said, "True, although I did use my Mossberg on him once. I used a slug round too. That's what caused the wound on the right side of his chest. He won't forgive me for that."

After Olivia said that, the creature gave a guttural growl and hissed, a combination of the roar of a bear followed by the hiss of an alligator. "It understood you," I said breathlessly.

"Of course," Olivia said. "He was human once upon a time. How long ago, I couldn't tell you. I bet it was well before your or my time. My grandparents probably weren't even born yet when he transformed into that."

"I don't understand. What's stopping him from killing us?"

Olivia pointed at the torches. "Fire has an interesting effect on his kind. I'm not sure if it can kill him. Then again, most things can't, but fire has some type of repelling force. It's like he can't walk close to it for some reason, even though legend doesn't exactly say that it can kill him. One thing is certain though: he's terrified."

I was trying to process what Olivia was telling me. The tall, grotesque being that stood before me was afraid of fire? The creature, according to God knows how many stories, was basically immortal, yet *fire* was his kryptonite? I struggled to believe it, but then I recalled the first time I saw the same creature. On the night he attacked Wyatt, it was far from where our makeshift campfire was. In fact, it was almost nothing but embers by the time he showed up. Even when Clare mentioned that she felt she was being followed and when Wyatt first encountered the beast, it all happened in the dark woods. Far away from the fire.

"Okay," I said. "But how do you know all this? Why is he here?"

Olivia sighed. "You and I might have a little more in common than you think."

"What do you mean?" I noticed the Wendigo then started to walk on all fours again and paced back and forth between the torches, as if looking for a way in. Olivia paid the monster no mind. She was so nonchalant about all of this, as if she had been through this situation many times before. She sat on the top step of the porch next to me as we both watched the enraged monster pacing outside the torch barrier.

"My parents left Alberta when I was a teenager. Since then, I spent most of my upbringing in Wyoming. I joined the Army for a few years, then took up nursing. Later on, I met Roy. After a few years, we got married and he talked me into moving out here after I retired. I knew back then that these woods felt ancient and had a strange aura about them. Like they were trying to hide something away from the rest of the world. Then one day I went out hunting for quail."

Her eyes dropped down as she thought. The Wendigo stopped pacing now and was sitting on his back legs like a dog. His empty eye sockets stayed locked onto us.

"I didn't catch anything that day," she continued, "so I ended up staying out late. When the sun started to set, I gave up and went home. On my way back, I heard something running at me. At first it was light and distant, then it kept getting closer and louder. I heard twigs snapping, leaves crunching, and then I heard the grunting and snarling. It sounded like a wild animal. I had a hunting rifle with me at the time, but when I saw him, I was too scared to even shoot. It looked just like how the elders in my home-town described it. And so I ran and ran. I shot back at him a few times. Didn't help, of course. Then I remembered when the elders told me how the Witiko are afraid of fire. When I made it to my house, Roy was still out at work. I ran into my living room and went for one of the air freshener cans and reached for the lighter in my pocket. When I turned, there he was. He was standing right in the center of my porch, snarling and grunting as he approached me. So I held the lighter in front of the air freshener, aimed and shot a big blast of flames at him. Mind you, I never did that before."

I stood with wide eyes as she continued explaining her first encounter with the Wendigo. I could see her eyes as she relived the horror she went through that day. I then asked,"Then what? Did he just keep coming back?"

"Well, he did run off that night, but it wasn't the last time I've seen him, and I knew what I had to do. The next day, I asked Roy to take me out to find some torches from the local market. I've bought over a dozen of them and we set them up around the house. I knew he thought I was crazy, but little did he know I was protecting us both. I haven't seen the Witiko too often since that day. At least until you showed up."

I looked down at her in shock and confusion. "What? You think he's here because of me?"

Olivia then turned to me with a sincere, don't-lie-to-me expression. "He took one of you, didn't he?"

I stared back, not sure if I should answer. "Don't lie," she warned. "There's been a lot of death in these woods. Your friend, Wyatt, is it? He wasn't the first."

"H-How did you…" I stuttered.

Olivia waved her hand to silence me. "I've been eavesdropping on you and your girlfriend. Naughty of me, I know. But you three are in deeper shit than you can imagine."

"I don't understand," I said, frustrated and confused.

"He made an offering to you, didn't he?"

"An offering? What the hell are you talking about, lady?"

"There's a part of the tale that didn't get passed down as much as the rest of the stories, but this part is important nonetheless. When a Witiko makes an offering to you, it will follow you until you take it. Usually, these offerings are the flesh of other humans."

That's when it all clicked. I remembered what it did to Wyatt. If the legends of the creature were true and it was truly cursed with eternal and insatiable starvation, then why would it leave out half of its kill in front of our van that night? Why wouldn't it just devour it like any other wild animal controlled by madness? And also, why didn't it just kill us that night? Looking at the Wendigo now in its full hulking form, I knew that it could've easily torn the van door off and killed the rest of us. Yet it didn't. Instead, it wanted to "share" its kill with us?

"But why?" I nearly stammered, realizing that there was so much about this monster that I clearly didn't understand. "Why would this thing want to share his kill with us and follow us all this way when he had a chance to kill us all along?"

I was waiting for Olivia to answer. But to my astonishment, that was when the Wendigo slightly straightened itself upward. Bones snapping and twisting as he moved, like a long-dead corpse forcing itself to reanimate. Then he spoke.

His voice was like a deep baritone filled with hate. I could hear it rumble and echo from the creature's maw and I felt the rage and impatience that clung to it as it reached my ears. And all he said was one word.

"JOIN," it groaned. Just as he spoke, he carried himself away on all fours and slowly crept back into the woods. He disappeared into the thickets while keeping his skull facing directly at me. In seconds, the shadowy darkness behind the tree line swallowed his body and face and he was gone.

I stood there in bewilderment, not sure what to make of what happened. My eyes scanned the trees in front of the home and the dirt road but caught no sign of the creature. I just knew there was no way he was gone just like that. This was far from over. The only thing that clung to my mind was that I had to get me and my friends out of that forest.

"Even if you leave now, he'll still find you," Olivia said, as if reading my thoughts. I guess the terror on my face said it all. "Witiko has been following you here. This might've been the second time you've seen him, but trust me, he hunts in the daylight too. How do you think he knew you were here?"

"Please. There's gotta be something we can do," I said. "You said he fears fire. Does that mean we can burn him?"

"It can," she admitted,"But it won't be enough to let you all escape. Your best option is–"

Before Olivia could finish her thought, she was interrupted by a loud crash, followed by something shattering like a thousand bits of glass landing on the floor. We both turned toward the sound and found it was coming from inside the house. We took quick, alarmed glances at each other when a loud, terrified scream came from the same direction as the crash. My blood ran cold when I recognized the scream. It was Sahrye.

I bolted top speed into the house with Olivia following beside me. We took a turn down the hallway where we saw Sahrye sitting on the floor whimpering and curled in an armadillo-like position as she covered her face. I started to run over when a gust of wintery air hit me from out of nowhere. I turned and faced the direction from where the thick flakes of snow were coming from, just to find they were coming from the room that was adjacent to the room we slept in. I remembered that it was the room Roy was sleeping in when I first passed through.

The large window in the room was completely broken, as if something bashed through with a battering ram. Broken glass and pieces of the window frame were all over the carpet. The cold air and snow rushed in, almost making me forget we were indoors. Something caught my eye when I looked towards the bed. The covers looked like they were forcibly ripped back and slightly torn apart, like someone slashed it with a machete. Then I saw something glistening on the sheets. It was blood. There was so much that the pillow and the mattress were soaked in it. I had to turn my head away immediately to keep myself from vomiting, but not because of the blood. It was because in the center of the thick blood stains was a torn human arm that still had strands of flesh connected to it. It looked like it was just recently torn directly out of someone's arm socket with brute force.

That was when Olivia ran into the room from behind me. She looked around the room as she took in the jaw-dropping sight. "Roy? Roy! Where are you? Are you here?" When her eyes dropped down to the decimated limb on the bed, she found her answer.

Her eyes began to fill with tears and she held her hand over her mouth as she realized what happened to her husband. She muttered something in her hand as she bolted out of the room but I couldn't make out what she was screaming. I took a step toward the window, which was now reduced into a hole in the wall. The outline was dented and cracked, as if whatever broke through it was so large that it had to forcibly squeeze itself in. Then I noticed deep claw marks were etched into the window seal.

If that wasn't alarming enough, I took notice of the deep footprints in the snow that led from the woods. Lying beside the tracks was one of Olivia's torch posts; the glass which was supposed to protect the flame was completely shattered, and the wooden pole looked as if it was hacked and broken from its base. I didn't know if it was possible, but my first thought was that someone purposely broke one of the torches.

I immediately decided that the house wasn't safe for any of us. I wasn't sure where Olivia ran to, and Roy was obviously taken by the Wendigo. There was no sign of the rest of his body, but based on what Olivia had told me, the torn arm still sitting on the bed was another offering. The monster was still trying to get us to eat his kill with him.

Sahrye was sitting on the floor with her knees close to her face. I knew then that she saw the creature, and she had to have watched it tear apart Roy while he was in his bed. Not only did she watch the Wendigo kill someone in real life, but I had a feeling that the arm wasn't just for the remaining survivors. He presented the offering to her specifically this time.

I quickly knelt down to her and shook her gently to get her to snap out of it. She looked up at me with shocked wide eyes. For the first time ever, at least for as long as I'd known her, she was actually terrified. "It talked!" she screamed with a panicked expression. "It killed him and looked at me and said, 'Join me.' It…it killed Roy, Aaron. It just pulled him apart like he was nothing!"

I shook her again until she looked into my eyes and I said, "We've got to go. Now!" As I spoke, her eyes darted from the blood-soaked bed and back at me. She then nodded and we both picked ourselves up and ran down the hall towards the front door. When we ran onto the porch, we saw that Roy's pickup truck was still sitting in the driveway. The plan seemed simple enough, but when we made it to the truck, we found the doors were locked.

"The key! Where's the key?" Sahrye screamed.

We're screwed, I thought. The torch circle was the only thing that kept the Wendigo from attacking us. Now that he found a way to tear down one of the torches, it was in the perimeter. It was only a matter of time before he found us again.

"Guys! Wait!" Me and Sahrye turned to the sound of someone running towards us. To our surprise, it was Clare. She ran toward us with something jiggling in her hand: the keys to the truck.

Sahrye stared in disbelief and yelled," Clare? Where were you? And how did you–"

She wasn't able to finish as Clare pushed past her to unlock the truck door. The doors made a clicking sound and we all quickly made our way into it. The seats were cold and we were able to see our breaths, but there we had no time to wait for it to warm up. Sahrye was the one who took the keys and went for the steering wheel, while me and Clare squeezed into the back. She twisted the key in the ignition and the truck whistled and groaned as its engine started.

"Where are we gonna go?" Sahrye asked.

"Anywhere but here," I yelled,"Now get us the fuck out of here!"

Sahrye put the truck in drive and circled out of the driveway. We were halfway down the dirt road when a large shadow appeared over the truck like a massive bird hovering over us in the snowy night sky. Me and Clare flinched when we first saw the shadow while Sahrye focused her attention on the snow-covered pathway. A nagging feeling kicked in the back of my head. Something in me knew we were driving into a trap. My hunch was proving correct when we made it around a curve on the pathway. Sahrye's eyes bulged as she immediately braked.

Standing a few feet in front of us was the Wendigo. He had followed us out of the driveway. Now me, Sahrye, and Clare sat frozen as the monstrosity "stared" back at us. Puffs of steam blew from his mouth with a quick rhythm like he was in the middle of running a marathon. I could see chunks of flesh hanging from the sides of his mouth. The monster pointed a bloody talon at us and with a deep, throaty voice, he said, "Join!"

I wanted to tell Sahrye to back up the truck, but I knew the truth now. Hell, we all did. It was over. This monster was more than just folklore. It was a supernatural being with abilities that we could barely fathom. Escaping was not an option now. We sat there for a while, waiting for the Wendigo to do something. We expected him to jump onto the truck and bash through the glass and tear each of us to pieces. But instead he just stood there. Then he turned his head to face the side of the truck. At first I thought he was trying to look at me or Sahrye or Clare, but then I saw another figure approach from behind the truck. The three of us gasped as Olivia emerged from up the path.

The Wendigo looked almost confused. I assumed that's how he felt judging on how he tilted his head as Olivia walked close. Her hands were wrapped around some type of weapon. At first, I thought it was a long hunting rifle, but as she walked in front of the truck's headlights, I saw that she had a large flamethrower. Her hands didn't shake and her bare feet sunk in the snow as she stood facing the beast. She was barely half the size of him but she showed no sign of fear as she looked up at the animal skull that glared down at her.

Olivia and the Wendigo stared at each other for a moment. Then the Wendigo opened his jaws and a voice called from within, like a trapped person calling from the depths of a cavern. The same deep, echoey voice I'd heard before slowly asked, "Have you decided? Will you join me?"

Olivia looked back at the beast with fury in her eyes. Her cheeks trembled as if she held back the urge to cry after everything she lost that night. She then screamed, "Never!"

She turned her head toward us and yelled at the top of her lungs, "Go! Now!" She then lifted the flamethrower and a jet of flames spewed out of the muzzle at the Wendigo. Sahrye put the truck in full speed and drove around the two. We saw one of the Wendigo's antlers catch on fire as more flames drizzled from the weapon. Sahrye continued driving as the snow-covered pathway led us to the highway. We rode on for a while, not sure if Olivia's flamethrower stunt was her last stand or if she was actually able to defeat the being.

It'd been almost a half-hour since we got on the highway. During that time, we probably passed a car every five minutes, so I assumed we were getting close to the interstate. None of us spoke about what we saw, although there probably wasn't a need to. Both of the girls witnessed for themselves that the creature I'd been describing was not only real, but was also hunting us. In these past few days, we'd learned there are things in this world that are beyond our understanding.

After what seemed like an eternity of hearing nothing but each other's fast, heavy breathing and the clattering of something underneath the old, rusted truck, Clare took a glance at me and Sahrye and sighed. "I-I think this is partially my fault," she said with guilt.

I figured she was trying to break the unnerving silence between us so I tried assuring her that everything from the car crash, to the snow-storms, to Wyatt and the Wendigo probably could've been avoided if I agreed to stay at the hotel for an extra night to wait out the first storm. I told her that we all probably had a piece of blame to share, but it all started with me. That was when she shook her head and said,"No. It's not just that. It's about the Wendigo."

Sahrye turned and looked at Clare from the driver's seat and said, "That thing was running around killing people long before we ever showed up in these woods. If it didn't hunt us, it would've just hunted another group of people eventually. Didn't Olivia say that it can live forever and that it's always hungry or whatever?"

I nodded, recalling the stories that Olivia told all three of us during lunch. And then I remembered what she told me when we were on the porch staring at the Wendigo behind the torch circle.

Clare's hands squeezed each other and she snapped,"No. There's more than that. Something happened at the crash site that I didn't tell you guys about yet."

This made my ears perk up. Sahrye was also looking back at Clare with suspicion. "Clare?" she carefully and slowly asked. "What happened?"

Clare was silent for a moment before continuing. Sahrye looked at her from the top mirror with a judgmental glare. Tears slowly started to collect and drip from her eyes as she reluctantly spoke. "Remember when I told you two about when I walked into the woods alone? When I said I felt something was following me, that's because something *was*."

I turned to Clare to make sure I was hearing her clearly. "So…you saw it, didn't you?"

I saw her eyes shift to see me from her peripheral and she nodded. I sat back, shocked, although part of me knew that her original story didn't exactly add up. Even Sahrye stared at her friend in disbelief. Before we could ask for more details, Clare continued and quietly sobbed as she talked.

"It followed me for a while. And I tripped over a rock or something and fell. I think that was why my wound started to open up under the old wrapping on my arm. When I turned around and looked up, there it was. I thought I was done for, especially with a busted arm and all. But then we both heard you guys yelling. I think the first person it heard was Wyatt."

By now, Clare's voice started to tremble and her eyes looked like they were about to melt. "And then it turned back at me. And it started talking. It sounded like it asked a question, but I couldn't tell at first. Then it asked the question again and--"

"It asked you to join?" I guessed.

Clare nodded, looking rather surprised that I knew. "It all happened so fast. I just shook my head to say yes. I didn't know what it meant or if those were the words it actually said. But after I said yes, it backed away. Like it instantly changed its mind about eating me. I thought it was gonna leave me alone but then Wyatt came." She hesitated after saying her fiancé's name and a flash of guilt took over her tear-stained face. "He saw it too. The Wendigo turned to look at him. It was about to ask him the same question, but Wyatt swung his flashlight against its head when it got close. Wyatt ran. And the Wendigo snarled and got pissed off. Then it followed him."

Sahrye looked at Clare and then me, probably piecing together the story I told about Wyatt's death, Olivia's story that she learned from her hometown, and now Clare's side of the story. Now it all made sense. Clare, whether by accident or otherwise, made a promise with the Wendigo that she would join it. Because of that, it probably wanted ALL of us to join. The only ones who refused were Olivia, Wyatt, and possibly Roy. Two of them were definitely dead, and the other was last seen shooting flames all over her property just to help us escape.

"I'm sorry. I'm so, so sorry," Clare sobbed.

Sahrye shook her head before saying, "You didn't know, Clare. We're almost out of this. It can't chase us all the way back to Denver."

I sat in silence when I thought about what my girlfriend had just said and I wondered. If I was an immortal being who's constantly hungry, and the only thing that could hurt me was fire, what would stop me from following a group of young adults across a state line or two? The distance and timing probably wouldn't mean anything. The same creature was probably circling around Olivia's protection circle for years, waiting for one of the torches to die out so it could sneak in and eat both her and her husband. That led me to another question to ask Clare.

"The torch circle. You knew about it, didn't you? Did you…break it on purpose?"

Sahrye scrunched her eyebrows in confusion. Of course, that was because Olivia didn't tell her about her early troubles with the Wendigo and how she convinced her husband to help her build the protective circle that kept them alive for years. Clare looked at me. Her shameful look answered my questions.

"I didn't know what the torches were for," she swore. "I thought they were some tribal custom shit or something Olivia did to remember her culture or whatever."

"Clare. Tell us what you did," I commanded. For a while, I've pitied Clare. At the start of this trip, she was a kind, humorous, life-of-the-party type of person. She was the type of extroverted friend that me or Sahrye would be grateful to have around at any social gathering. But after watching her endure her broken arm and the sudden death of her fiancé, I watched as the bubbly, passenger-seat DJ became a broken, cowardly woman. Before, I was hesitant to probe her for more answers, but I'd had enough. If she had something to do with the death of two strangers and sending a monster on our trail, then I wanted nothing but the truth.

Clare nodded as she understood the sincerity in my tone and said, "It came to me again. It happened a couple hours ago, when I was on the couch. I heard it calling me. It was outside the house groaning, saying, 'Join. Join.' And it said it over and over again. I don't know why, but I got up, got dressed, and went out the front door looking for it. I walked around the house. I don't know how long I was out there, but when I was about to walk back in, I heard you and Olivia walk out. I didn't want to worry you guys or look suspicious so I hung around the chicken coop on the side of the house. Then I heard the Wendigo again. I followed it farther, near the back of the house, until I saw it. At first I felt angry, like I wanted to hurt it after knowing what it did to Wyatt. Then I felt…helpless. Like there's no point in living, you know. I got close to it, expecting it to rip my throat out or something. But no, it just stood behind one of the torches and looked at me. Then it pointed at the torch and said, 'Fire. End it. Let me in.' I had an idea what it was trying to say, but I hesitated. Then it asked if I still wanted to join."

"No," I said, hoping what I was hearing wasn't true. "Please tell me you didn't listen to it."

Clare took a deep breath before answering. "I took some snow and dumped it on one of the torches. When the fire died, it stood up and swiped at the torch pole, splitting it in two. Then it ran past me and crawled up to one of the windows. I heard crashing, a bunch of people screaming and…"

Clare trailed off as she looked at both me and Sahrye.

"You got Roy killed," Sahrye said with a cracking voice. Clare stared at her hands in shame with the realization of what she had done. From that point, I didn't know what to say. On one hand, I almost felt sympathetic, knowing that Clare was willing to give up her life out of hopelessness. On the other hand, she did cause Roy and Olivia to become the Wendigo's new victims, also endangering us in the process. The inside of the vehicle was silent again and we avoided eye contact.

After a while, I noticed a sign indicating that we were getting close to a junction where the current road and the interstate met. I pointed to the signs and told Sahrye to follow them. A moment later we made a couple turns that led to a ramp to the interstate. Suddenly I saw a blur of darkness and bone from the corner of my eye. Before I could scream or yell, it was too late. The next thing we knew, we were met with a heavy mass of dark fur, bones, muscle, and antlers, followed by brute force and rage. The truck flipped over the guardrail and off the ramp. It flipped once more before landing on its top, forcing us to scramble.

We all hurried to reach the doors to escape when the sound of hooved feet came in our direction. We turned just as a pair of long ebony claws stabbed their way into the door and ripped it away with ease. There it was: the snarling face of the Wendigo. One of his antlers was darker than the other after being scorched earlier. It reached one of his long, sinewy arms into the truck and grabbed Sahrye from the driver's seat. She screamed and scratched at the massive hand that wrapped around her and began to yank her away. Me and Clare yelled for Sahrye until the beast returned. This time he reached with both claws and yanked us both out of the flipped truck.

The last thing we saw was the beast hauling all three of us over his shoulders holding us in place with his giant claws while his hooved feet ran through the woods. I saw nothing but passing shadows of the night as the monster pushed through the trees and thickets. I heard him huff and grunt as he ran and leaped. I couldn't help myself; I felt my eyes slowly close as I began to faint.

Have you ever had a fever dream? A dream that left you with an intense feeling after you woke up? That's what I felt when I awoke. I found myself arching forward, fighting to catch my breath and my awareness back.

The first thing I noticed was the rocky, slightly jagged surface my body was lying on. I turned my head and saw that I was sitting in a clearing. It was still dark out, but I could see the outline of the trees in the distance in the moonlight. The clearing, as far as I could see, was a rocky surface. Contrasted to the rest of the forest, the area was barren, as though this patch of land hasn't seen vegetation or life in a long time.

I turned and noticed that bodies surrounded me. I jumped when I recognized Sahrye and Clare lying unconscious on either side of me. I shook them both, fearing they were dead. To my relief, Sahrye was the first to jolt awake, followed by Clare, who immediately gazed around the clearing and asked where we were. I told them I didn't have a clue.

We were moments away from getting to our feet when something caught our attention. We froze as the sound of slow, heavy footsteps approached us from the darkness. A moment later, we watched as the Wendigo's skull emerged into the moonlight while the rest of his body seemed to be shrouded by darkness. He carried something over his shoulder. It was difficult to see what it was; all we knew was that it looked heavy and limp. Then the creature flung the thing, forcing it to slam into the stony ground with a sickening thud. The thing rolled over, and we could see it was Olivia. Her eyes were partially shut, and there was a large gaping cavity in the side of her abdomen, like a massive bite was taken out of her. She was dead, there was no doubt about that. Seeing her like this after meeting her only half a day ago was so disturbing.

The three of us sat and watched in petrified disgust and terror as the Wendigo dug his claws into Olivia's flesh. It made a grotesque crunching sound as he tore into the flesh and yanked out pieces in front of us. Then he held up the scraps of meat above our heads, like he was granting us a benevolent gift. He presented a piece of the flesh to Clare. She shuddered and whimpered as she stared at the chunky blob of flesh that sent a steady stream of blood from the monster's claws. He brought his skull-face close to Clare's. His snout was merely an inch away when it asked the same question it asked many times before.

"Join?"

Clare looked at the monster and then us in confusion, although, based on how he gestured the flesh to her, we were all certain what he wanted her to do. Clare looked at the flesh for a long moment. Eventually, she closed her teary eyes, shuddered and she slowly opened her mouth. For the first time since we'd been awake, I noticed something else was in the clearing with us. All around us were deep carvings in the ground; markings of characters I wasn't familiar with. They reminded me of the ancient runes and cuneiform from tablets and monuments that were discovered and mentioned on the History Channel. But these symbols were large and looked to be older than the forest itself.

The next thing that happened was unexplainable, but as the Wendigo brought the flesh closer to Clare's mouth, the markings surrounding us began to glow with orange, whimsical light. Soon, the Wendigo placed a handful of flesh into Clare's mouth and gently used one of his talons to close her mouth, urging her to chew and swallow his offering. Clare looked like she was on the verge of vomiting, but she stopped herself, knowing that doing so would most likely upset the Wendigo and that she would simply become another victim of his wrath. By then, the runes were so bright that they lit the entire clearing around us, revealing everyone.

The Wendigo's mouth slightly opened as he watched Clare struggle to consume his offering. It was as if he was managing to smile through his bloodied, jagged teeth. Clare dropped to her hands and knees as she chewed on the flesh to make the portions small enough to swallow without vomiting.

After an intense struggle, all we heard was a rough gulping sound from her throat as she swallowed the flesh. Afterward she began gasping for air, and I saw something in her eyes begin to change. She looked down at the small puddle of blood that had formed on the ground when the Wendigo first approached her. Her pupils slowly began to expand and her bloody mouth curled into a smile, her tongue dangling out like a panting dog. A moment later, me and Sahrye watched in horror and disgust as Clare threw herself onto her hands and knees and began to lap up Olivia's blood with her entire tongue like a dehydrated hound drinking water, making heavy gasping sounds. We saw the crazed look on her face as she licked the blood off of the ground. It was like something in her switched and turned her into a wild animal.

Sahrye sobbed as she tried calling her friend's name but Clare ignored her and continued licking up the blood like it was the most delicious thing on earth. This was one of the most disturbing things we'd both seen so far, but the nightmare was only beginning. The Wendigo returned to Olivia's corpse and ripped out another chunk of bleeding flesh, this time from her thigh. He then approached Sahrye, while holding the flesh with one of his claws in a polite manner. A part of me wanted to give the creature a strong left hook, but I knew that was futile. We were all his playthings now. Whatever the reason was for sharing his kill with us, we had no choice but to partake and prepare for whatever happened next. To refuse would only mean becoming the next meal. Sahrye seemed to understand that by now. She looked at the slimy red strands of meat that the Wendigo brought closer to her face. The monster glared down at her and asked, "Join?"

Sahrye said nothing but slowly opened her mouth. A stream of tears ran down from her eyes to her cheeks as the human flesh was gently placed into her mouth. After the Wendigo pushed her chin upward, she gasped. Just like Clare, she struggled chewing at first. Then her pupils began to dilate and a smile slowly grew across her face. A minute later, she was chewing the rest of the portion with even less resistance. After a few swift gulps, she crawled on her hands and knees and began licking up the corpse's blood alongside Clare.

The Wendigo returned to the corpse a third time and tore a large chunk of viscera from the chest area. When he approached me, I recognized the body part he wanted me to eat. It was Olivia's heart. It lay limp in the center of his large clawed hands as he brought it closer to my face. "Join," he commanded in a deep, echoey voice like a phantom. I stood still and said nothing, not sure if he expected me to respond knowing that I had no options. But he tilted his head as if he actually wanted me to respond before giving me the offering. "Join?" He asked, this time with a tone that was filled with malice and impatience. It was clear now that he didn't just want to give me an offering but also wanted to see me submit while doing so. The only way I could survive now would be to admit defeat. And so I did.

I was reluctant, but I nodded in agreement. The Wendigo then brought the heart to the front of my mouth and I took a deep bite into it. The texture was thick, the taste strange and metallic, and it took a while to chew. I covered my mouth to keep myself from spitting it out. Every cell in my body was telling me that this was wrong and absolutely disgusting, but I reminded myself that it was either this or death.

After I swallowed, I felt a tingling sensation trickle across my brain. Goosebumps began to form across my arms, cheeks, and legs. My tongue began to twitch as the flavor of the flesh in my mouth began to…change me. It was as if as soon as I swallowed the first chunk, I became addicted. No, "addicted" was an understatement. My brain screamed to me that I needed more and that nothing else in the world mattered more than taking another bite. So I did. I took a larger, stronger bite, chewed and swallowed quickly. Then I did it again, and again, and again. In a few seconds, the heart was gone. All that was left was blood stains on my hands and face. I sniffed at them and moaned in ecstasy.

I found myself licking my hands as if they were coated in birthday cake frosting. I couldn't believe what I was doing, but the flesh and blood that severely grossed me out just moments ago, was now the only thing I wanted. It was the only thing I could think of, and I wanted, no…I NEEDED more. Before I knew it, I, too, was on the ground next to Sahrye and Clare licking at the puddle of blood.

Eventually, we made our way to the remaining corpse itself and began to indulge. Then the Wendigo got on all fours and joined us in the feast. Suddenly all four of us surrounded the human corpse and tore and bit into every piece of flesh that was left. I didn't even remember leaving the bones behind.

After that, everything was a blur. It was like we'd walked into a nightmare, even though we all knew that everything that happened after that night was real. It was like we were reborn.

From then on, we followed the Wendigo, which sounded absolutely insane knowing what he made us do but at the same time we felt obligated. Somehow we knew that he'd feed us again. During the first few days of following him, he led us to a small campsite: an average sized polyester tent with a campfire sitting in the front of it. There were two male campers who sat around the fire with sausages skewered on sticks and a kettle hanging over the flames. They looked at the flames and conversed, completely unaware of our presence, maybe it's because the Wendigo was crouching so close to the ground that the protruding spinal bones on his back were barely visible behind the bushes. Like lion cubs watching their mother hunt, we trailed behind, steadying our breathing and making soft, careful steps while we crawled on our knees and elbows.

The four of us sat in silence for a while, in the shadows behind the trees while peering at the two campers through the thorny leaves of the bushes.

After a long wait, the Wendigo leaped from the bushes and charged at the campers. The way he ran was startling enough. He switched between running on all fours, then on two legs, only to drop and gallop on all fours again.

One of the campers screamed and tried to scramble away from the Wendigo while the other pulled out a pistol and fumbled with it to find an accurate aim. Unfortunately for him, the Wendigo was on top of him a millisecond later, using his wolf-like fangs to rip into the camper's neck. Blood spewed out against the Wendigo's face like a split water hose as he violently whipped his head side to side to tear deeper into the flesh. I thought I heard a gunshot in the middle of the scuffle, although even if the camper did let loose an accurate shot, it would be futile and his fate wouldn't change.

After the first camper fell limp, the other camper panicked and pushed his way into the tent and struggled to close it up. Unfortunately, he was barely able to zip up the flap halfway before the beast leaped onto him, causing them both to stumble backwards. We didn't see the two after they collapsed into the tent, but we watched as the tent was tossed around back and forth until it fell on its side. There was a loud, blood-curdling scream, followed by the sound of something wet crashing and thudding. There was a silence that followed, but we still didn't dare to move a muscle. For some inexplicable reason, we felt compelled to wait.

A moment later, the Wendigo dragged the two bodies of the campers into the woods where we stood. The Wendigo then made a feverish, ravenous sound before forcing his teeth and claws into the corpses to feed. Sahrye and Clare immediately crawled towards the bodies and began to tear pieces of the flesh apart, quickly tossing them into their mouths. A part of me felt disgusted at the sight: the crazed, bug-eyed look both girls had as they dug their bloody fingers into the corpse like it was the best thing they ever ate. I wanted to leave, to run far away from this place and these people who I once loved.

I looked at Sahrye as she ate and I barely recognized her, yet before I knew it, I was drawn to the corpses like a magnet. I lost all control over my body when my own hands began to pull the flesh away from the bones. My mouth watered as I looked at the parts that should've grossed me out and I began tearing away pieces of the body and eating them.

A new part of me took hold; a part that was new but at the same time primal, ancient, and undeniable. It had the last word, and it forced my body to keep eating while instilling in me the promise that whatever part I was chewing on would cure the powerful, aching hunger-pains that took a hold of me. But it didn't. Instead, after every bite I took, my mind slipped further away. It was like I was doing something completely against my will, yet the more I did it, the more my mind became blank. Within moments of eating, my rational mind was absent, leaving behind nothing but instinct and hunger. Eventually, I was a mindless animal completely governed by hunger pains, instincts, and emotional thrills. And I loved it.

I couldn't tell you how long we continued the new routine. It had to have been weeks, if not months, since we started following the Wendigo. There were no rulebooks or guidelines presented to us to follow while carrying on this lifestyle, but one thing that felt almost innate and definite was that the Wendigo was the leader of our group now. He was our alpha and he knew everything about the ancient forests. He knew where the deer herds were grazing, when the large flocks of geese would arrive at a nearby lake, and where to find the campsites and RV lots where unsuspecting humans were.

It turned out that the stories Olivia and others told about the Wendigo were missing a minor detail. The Wendigo wasn't exactly picky about what he hunted and ate. Although human flesh was a delicacy, they weren't the only things we saw him hunt. There were times when we would track herds of deer, flocks of geese and even trout and salmon in the nearby rivers. When we did hunt humans, it was always at night, right when the sun was no longer in view. And when I said "we", I was being literal. For a while we only sat in the bushes and watched as our alpha crept through the shadows while following a lone, straggling human who was taking a piss or sight-seeing in the night. Then of course, right when the hairs on their neck would stand up as they realized something was following them, our Alpha was already on top of them, sealing their fate to become our next meal.

After watching him hunt a dozen times, the rest of us eventually began to take the initiative on the hunts. We would take turns each night, but Sahrye was the first to hunt down a human. It was a woman who was tending to her water reservoir for her RV one night. Sahrye crouched low as she snuck around the RV and up behind the woman. I still remembered the look in her eyes as she did this; they had a relentless, laser focus to them, as if nothing in the world could distract her. When the woman turned around and noticed Sahrye stalking behind her, she was startled for a moment. Then the shock turned into a sympathetic and alarming concern.

"Ma'am, are you okay? Are you camping out here too? Do you need help? You don't look well, hon," the woman asked calmly as Sahrye simply just stared at her. Sahrye, like the rest of us, was covered in filth and mud all over her clothes. Leaves and pieces of wood clung to her messy, raven-black hair.

When the woman realized something was off about Sahrye, she turned away and said, "Stay right here. I'm going to get help." She was probably going back to her RV to contact a local ranger or patrolling officer by radio or phone to let them know that a strange, wild-looking young woman was walking around alone.

Unfortunately, just as the woman turned to open the RV's door, Sahrye charged at her back and tackled her to the ground. The two women fought against each other in the grass. While the woman was yelling and pushing away, Sahrye was growling like a mangy dog, pulling the woman in closer. Then she brought her face close to the woman's throat and began biting down hard with all her jaw strength onto her windpipe.

The woman tried to scream but Sahrye continued tearing at her body until she was too weak to move. When the woman fell limp, Sahrye turned to the bushes to look at us and smiled with blood and saliva dripping from her lips and teeth. The alpha approached Sahrye and slowly brought his bony forehead close to hers. For a brief moment, they bowed and lightly touched their foreheads together before withdrawing and closing in around the corpse. Sahrye had been acknowledged by the alpha.

After seeing this, I felt it was my turn to get acknowledged by our master. I found my kill when a human was fishing near a local river the next night. He stood on the edge of the riverbank with a LED light connected to his hat to see. I won't go into details on how I hunted the fisherman but it was difficult tackling a man on a slippery edge. Luckily for me, the current in the river was weak but the water was deep enough for me to force the man's face into the water until he ran out of air. When I returned to the group with my kill, the alpha nodded at me with approval and we all feasted that night.

Clare was the last to find a kill. She came upon a hobo stumbling around near the highway. It was an older man with a scraggly beard and tattered clothes that had a heavy stench of urine. When Clare brought his body to us, a leg was missing and the neck was torn to the inner bone. It wasn't the best meal we had but we didn't neglect what she was able to score for the family.

We had pretty much forgotten our old lives. I would occasionally see flashes and hints of the past; when I first met Sahrye, the trips we took, first meeting Clare and driving in the snow. I thought I remembered something about a guy who was with us at one point but I couldn't really remember his name. Hell, I couldn't even remember my own name.

We were still able to talk, although we didn't see the need to. We would utter or grunt a word every now and then, but mostly we got our points across by growling, snarling, whimpering, and sometimes screaming if we needed to. Other than that, it was usually our alpha who did most of the talking, although he never spoke in complete sentences either. He would only speak with a couple of words, though he often used one in a commanding and ghastly tone. He would simply point in a direction and yell,"Follow," and we would instantly follow him. When he brought us a kill, he would say, "Feed," and we would do so.

Our speech, memories, and our minds were quickly altered, but our bodies began to change shortly after. It all started with the rash. Me, Sahrye, and Clare each noticed weird red bumps that started on our legs and arms. Soon the rash reached our necks and faces, where the itching sensation was the most excruciating. Many times, after scratching at the hives, there would be pieces of my own skin hanging from my fingernails, like scratching plastic and duct tape off a box. I remembered scratching my head one day and feeling something rough and hard like sharp pebbles sticking from the top of my head. When I ran to a lake to look at my reflection, I stared in disbelief at the small protrusions. They were horns! I had small horns growing out of my skull. I also noticed my nails grew longer and faster than usual and the skin of my face and neck began to fade and peel away. I would slide my tongue across my teeth as I ate, and felt that they had grown longer and sharper. Eventually, I had to figure out a new way to chew my meals without chomping my own tongue off.

This transformation took hold of the three of us for about a week. I noticed that Clare's skin began to fall away from her face, revealing patches of bone and rotted flesh. I saw her head starting to sprout horns just like mine. After a while, we started to take notice of our new forms after a hellish period of scratching our skin away and feeling our bones and muscles twist and stretch in the most unnatural ways imaginable.

One day, after the pain and the itchy sensations stopped, I decided to crawl to the edge of the lake to see my reflection again. I noticed just by standing up that something was wrong. I was taller, at least by another two feet, and my head even felt a bit heavier than I remembered.

I nearly stumbled and fell while adjusting to my new height and almost shrieked when I saw my reflection. My face was completely gone; to be more accurate, the *skin* on my face was gone. My entire head and neck consisted completely of exposed bone. The worst part was that my skull wasn't even a human skull anymore. It was now in the shape of an elongated and narrow skull resembling that of a sheep or a ram. On the top of my reflection's head were two massive black horns that curled like the horns on a ram. My teeth, however, looked like they belonged to something carnivorous, like a wild dog, with two larger fangs in the front that barely fit in my mouth.

One day, I awoke to find that my eyes were gone, but my vision was just the same as before. I couldn't remember when or how they fell out of the sockets but the feeling of their absence never dawned on me until I saw my reflection later on. Other than my sight that somehow remained the same, my sense of smell and hearing were better than before, despite my nose and ears being absent, reduced to empty cavities in my new head.

My nails were pitch-black claws that were each over three inches long and my skin was riddled with strange protrusions. Some of them were bones, others were veins and sinew with scattered patches of dark woolly fur. My clothes hung from my enlarged body like ripped pieces of cloth and my feet looked like they'd escaped my shoes long ago. Instead of toes and soles, they were large two-toed hooves that struck the dried leaves and mud beneath me.

As for Sahrye and Clare, they went through similar changes. They grew taller, became slightly hunched, and had large claws that grew from their hands. Clare's transformation, however, gave her the skull of a feline to re-place her human head. The skull resembled that of a leopard or a puma, with small dragon-like horns poking from the back where her ears would be. Her feet were dark paws that gripped the ground as she walked, and her arms were so abnormally long that they dragged across the ground even when she walked bipedally. Her arm that was broken before seemed to be fully functional after the bones and muscles morphed into their new shape.

Sahrye's new form was a tall, slender, abominable being with the head of a deer or antelope, almost like our alpha. The difference was that her head had sprouted long, pitch-black horns that pointed like scimitars in the air. It was clear now that our alpha's plan was complete. We were now officially part of his new tribe–a tribe of Wendigos.

By now, you would probably ask me," Wait, Aaron. If you are a Wendigo with no human memory or speech, then how are you telling this story?" Well, I guess the best way to explain would be by calling my final transformation a "rebirth." Think of it like this: Do you remember the day when you were born? Probably not. Even if you did, there would only be flashes of what happened that day. The same could be said for the entire time you were an infant. Afterall, they say babies can remember specific information by the time they're nine months old. Well, it's almost the same for me, only the flashes of memories I'd receive would be from my life as a human. Somehow, I was able to access the hidden memories from my past life later on.

Since the final transformation, the world was different. Everything was loud and clear. We were able to smell and hear animals and humans from over a mile away. None of us had eyeballs in our sockets anymore, but apparently that was irrelevant because we were still given much better eyesight than ever before. We could even see in the dark, and the things that were shrouded in the shadows appeared to us just as clear as they did in broad daylight. Despite spending most of our time hunched on all fours, we were all incredibly fast and nimble. Our height and strength combined with our speed and agility immediately slid us to the top of the food chain. Being the new apex predators allowed us to take down almost every prey we pursued, especially when we hunted as a group.

The one reason things took a sour turn was due to the hierarchy. Ever since we ate our first human corpse, our alpha has been our guide and he had the final word on any discussion. In fact, we rarely had discussions at all. Our alpha only spoke in forceful gestures, snarls, and commands with as few words as possible. This worked out fine when we were rookie hunters still undergoing our transformations, gradually slipping between humans and immortal beasts. But when we changed into our new bodies, the relationship also began to change. Since we were full Wendigos, we didn't depend on the alpha to lead the hunt. Each of us basically hunted whenever and wherever we wanted. The alpha was fine with this, but he uttered one rule in regards to our newfound freedom. "Your kill is OUR kill," he would grunt with a toothy scowl.

We all followed this rule. All of us except Sahrye, unfortunately. It seemed that even as a Wendigo, she didn't lose her rebellious personality. In fact, now that she was an apex predator that couldn't die, she was now emboldened to be rebellious.

Out of the three of us, it was Sahrye who was the most successful hunter. You see, I was the largest and strongest of the three of us while Clare was the smallest and somewhat more agile than me, allowing her to chase any prey, even if they were hiding in a tight space. Sahrye, however, had both advantages. She was smaller and more agile than I was, but she was also stronger and had a more muscular build than Clare. When me and Clare were unsuccessful in our hunts, Sahrye would track down and bring back a meal by using tactics which we lacked. Whenever a human, or larger game was able to outrun me or slip from my claws, there she was, intercepting them within the blink of an eye just when they thought they'd escaped.

We didn't take issue with Sahrye's success. There was no need for jealousy when we're constantly hungry. She was almost like the breadwinner of the family, which was fine with us as long as we were able to feed on something to hold back the eternal, painful hunger. Our alpha, however, took issue when she took down a hunter who was returning to his cabin. When he heard Sahrye stalking him, he took his hunting rifle and shot a bullet through her leg. When this failed to slow her down, she pounced on the hunter and tore into his chest, chewing his heart out. Me and Clare arrived to join her as she began gnashing on the bloody organ and pulling out his entrails.

At the time, our alpha was hunting on his own and didn't return to us until later that night. When he did, the first thing he saw was the three of us eating our meal without him. This was enough to infuriate him. Enraged after finding that we broke one of his rules, he ran after us while snarling and growling louder than I'd ever heard him before. He slammed his large fists into the ground, sending a shockwave throughout the forest floor around us. Me and Clare instinctively lowered ourselves on all fours in an almost bowing stance. We knew we'd disobeyed one of his rules and we made ourselves silent and small, bracing ourselves for severe punishment in return for disrespecting our master.

Our alpha stood on his rear legs and glared down at us. His menacing, ancient, massive form towered over us, sending a shadow that covered both me and Clare. He took an intimidating step forward while huffing and snarling angrily like a mad dog. Then, after landing one of his giant, stallion-like hooves inches away from my keeling head, he yelled, "Move!"

Clare and I didn't hesitate. We immediately scampered away from the corpse to allow our alpha to feast. Then the unexpected happened. Sahrye took a bold and abrupt step between the alpha and her kill. She bared her fangs and snarled at him, causing her long, needle-shaped horns to rattle on her skull. The alpha took a step back. For a brief moment, he was just as shocked as we were to see Sahrye act in this manner toward him. Then he caught himself, reminding himself that HE was the leader of the group. He created this tribe, and he'd be damned if he'd relinquish control now to a Wendigo that was much smaller and less seasoned than he was. He took a large, thunderous step forward and bared his fangs back at Sahrye while looking down directly at her. She didn't back down. Instead, she looked up at our alpha with her eyeless skull face, still baring her fangs.

The alpha realized what Sahrye was doing. She was challenging him. To him, this was the ultimate betrayal and disrespect. He now had no other choice but to make an example out of her. Without warning, he held one of his claws in the air and brought it down in a swift, hammer-like motion onto Sahrye's head. The blow sent Sahrye straight to the ground. The alpha didn't allow her to move or recover. Instead, just as she landed onto the ground, he grabbed her by the back of her neck and struck her in the chest with his knee with a force that made her bellow in agony. He immediately grabbed her by her neck again and tossed her aside, causing her to roll on her back and whimper.

After the alpha struck Sahrye and threw her aside, he returned to the corpse to eat his fill. He began dipping his face into the hunter's open chest cavity and started crunching down on his ribs, making a sloppy snapping sound as he ate in a frenzy. While he did this, me and Clare sat a few feet away at a safe distance and looked at Sahrye. She slowly turned her head in our direction while she lay on her back. Somehow I knew she was looking directly at me; her eyeless antelope skull, pointing in my direction, showed so much sorrow and defeat. Then she slowly opened her jaw and I heard a small, delicate, mournful voice echo from it.

"A-Aaron." It was like a familiar voice calling to me from inside a cavern. Since our transformation, I didn't actually remember my name, or any of our names. We were all just parts of a unit; mindless cogs destined to be part of the alpha's machine. I wasn't sure why or how she was able to say my name or even remember it, but whatever power allowed her to do so took hold of me too. Then it hit me. My memories flooded back to me.

I remembered how we got into the woods in the first place. I remembered the kind-hearted people we've met; the same ones who basically died so we could survive. I remembered that we weren't always like this.

We were humans once. I remember Wyatt, Roy, Olivia. We had other friends too. We had families who are probably worried to death about us. We had lives, adventures, love, and friendship and...

My thoughts stopped when I remembered how we became what we were. I remembered how the devil which we'd so foolishly called our "alpha" had taken everything from us. He had taken our lives, our friends and our own humanity. Now we were damned for all of eternity because of his fiendish games. It was then, after everything clicked, that I decided he had made his final mistake. After forcing us to become part of his tribe, he shared with us all of his abilities. Finally, I decided to use mine.

I turned toward the alpha, who was now chewing through the abdomen of the corpse. His disgusting, bony snout wiggled as he forced his way into the flesh. I felt a surge of rage take hold of me and before I could think, my legs and claws began ripping at the cold, frosted leaves and grass as I charged at the beast. He turned in astonishment just as I pounced on top of him, raking my claws across his skull, his chest and his back with all my fury.

As the Wendigo snapped and realized what was happening, he turned and bit down hard on my arm. I yelped as I felt his fangs sink their way through my bones. As it turned out, being immortal doesn't mean you get to live an endless, pain-free life. Though your lifespan could be eternal, you would still feel pain. Immortality was never a gift for the Wendigo, but instead a curse. You were a human soul locked away in a bony, putrid, half-human/half-animal abomination as a form of punishment. Looking at the Wendigo as we fought, I noticed all the old wounds that had been inflicted ages ago. Although the soul could technically "live" forever, the vessel could still be damaged, and pain, especially the pain of eternal hunger, was the only thing that could accompany you during your punishment for disobeying the laws of nature. While realizing all of this, I had an idea.

I tried using my other hand to pry the Wendigo's teeth out of my arm. When they didn't budge, I swung my hooves into the beast's shin, and then his groin. This finally caused him to stagger back and loosen his bite a little. I continued to use my hooves and free arm to make as many strikes as possible to get my other arm free. That was when another pair of claws came from behind the Wendigo and clung onto one of his antlers.

I turned and watched in awe as Clare used her claws to pull on the antler while using her rear, cat-like paws to grapple onto the monster's back. This caused him to release my arm and give a loud, echoey roar that reverberated across the forest. Clare's razor-sharp claws gave a strong pull downward, ripping the antler straight out of his head, leaving a trail of black, viscous fluid dripping from the bottom of it. Enraged after realizing what Clare had done to him, the Wendigo snarled and slammed into Clare with an immense force. She let out a cry that sounded like a furious jaguar as her body was sent into a nearby tree. Splinters and wood chunks clattered to the ground as Clare's back slammed into it.

I looked back at the Wendigo and saw that he was now holding his head in agony, trying to feel for his missing antler. I took my last chance. I pounced on top of him again; this time I reached directly for his deer skull. I clenched my claws around his face until I was able to get my thumbs into his eye sockets. The Wendigo roared with rage and pain as he frantically slammed his fists into my ribs. I mustered all my strength into my claws and kept a grip around the inner edge of the eye sockets.

I grunted and strained as I pulled my claws away from each other while holding the sockets tight. I pulled and pulled until suddenly I heard a loud, wet, cracking sound, like a large egg being split into pieces. I stopped and realized the Wendigo wasn't screaming and punching me anymore. I looked down at what I'd done, and my heart nearly skipped a beat. In each of my large, claw-like hands was a separate half of the Wendigo's head, each oozing a thick, black substance that smelled like sun-baked roadkill.

I looked at the ground as the body stumbled and limped away without its head. It bumped into a tree, then another, before stumbling away into the darkness like a drunkard. I took one last look at the split pieces of the Wendigo's skull in my claws and crushed them both at once, letting a blob of black ooze and bits of bones drizzle to the ground. Clare and Sahrye limped toward me and looked at the remains of our defeated master. That night we rejoiced and decided to go on another hunt to celebrate. We didn't find any more humans; however, we did manage to score a couple cattle from a farm we stumbled upon after galloping through the forests for a few miles.

After that night, we actually found a liking for cows that lived on the farms. Then we developed a craving for chicken, then goats. Things got problematic when the humans who owned the farms started noticing their horses had gone missing, so we eventually had to relocate.

The good news was, we were able to leave humans off the menu, at least for now. With the alpha gone, we could pretty much do whatever we wanted and go wherever we pleased. We soon were able to start talking again. At first we would only say each other's names; later, we were able to form sentences. They weren't as good as when we had actual human minds but it was better than grunting and snarling to communicate.

This evening, the three of us were watching the sunset. Sahrye nudged me under my chin and rested her head on my shoulder. "Aaron," her voice echoed.

"Yes," I responded, gently rubbing her back as we looked toward the gold and fiery glow in the sky, sending a purplish haze that gradually grew as night snuck its way around us.

"Is this…life now?" she asked. I'll admit, it was still kinda hard to accept being a monster after knowing you had a human life you were forced to leave behind. Yes, our new abilities were cool and all, but we left so much behind and there was no guarantee that we would ever return to our previous lives.

I knew the circumstances of our new reality could be tough for Sahrye to get used to, especially after getting her memories back. So, when I answered I said, "Yes. But life still same, just like before alpha. Because we together before, and we together now."

Even though a Neanderthal would have spoken better English than me, Sahrye nudged me again, because she understood what I was saying. I heard a laugh echo from her as we sat together. Clare came to sit with us shortly after. With her jaws, she brought us a decapitated boar to eat.

"Wanted to kill bigger," she said, her guilty voice echoing from her feline skull. It was like hearing a child complaining from the bottom of a well. "But I smell them again."

"Who?" Sahrye asked.

"Humans. Not farmers. The ones with big guns. Me think military."

Me and Sahrye looked at each other with concern. For about a week now, there had been a new scent in the woods we had decided to make a home in. We knew there were humans here but these were different. These humans wore all-black military attire. They had guns, but they didn't look like assault rifles or any guns the military would normally carry. They looked like large, silvery cannons that could easily leave us with massive wounds.

The last time we spotted one of them, they saw me and Sahrye hunting. We were able to outrun them before they called their fellow troops. I'm not sure how long they were in these woods or if they came to look for us specifically, but regardless, we'd been through too much to run forever. We'd eventually have to make ourselves known and prove to them why we were the apex predators in this forest. I didn't know when that would be, but I knew it was soon, because I could already smell them. And their scent was making me hungry.

STORY 2:

I SPOKE TO THE GUARD OF HADES

They say death is just another part of life. Just like everyone else, I had witnessed death, or at least lost a few loved ones in the past. My grandparents on both sides of my family passed away when I was still in my early teens. I lost my calico cat, Coco, to a Dodge Ram after she ran into a busy street on a Saturday morning when I was seven. Ever since I was young, death was never a stranger to me, but nothing prepared me for the distressing experience I'd sat through as my beloved wife died.

Her name was Charlotte. We met sometime in senior year of high school and although we were very close since we first met, we didn't officially start dating until almost a decade later. I'm not sure why it took so long for the two of us to become a couple. Perhaps it was because we were almost always in a relationship with other people, yet we always hung around in the same social circles with the same friends and did the same activities. Even when we were young, a part of me knew she was the woman I was destined to be with.

Her brilliant blue eyes always seemed to detect my soul whenever our eyes met. Her choice of perfume was almost intoxicating to me and her childish laugh was so contagious that I would often laugh along with her just from hearing her giggle. She often felt insecure about her red hair; she would complain about how frizzy it would get in warm weather and found it difficult to tame the thick, curly texture. I always found her hair alluring and kinky. I guess it depended on the angle. She would often wear a beanie to cover it, until one day I convinced her to wear it out. She was reluctant at first and she swore that her hair was too wild to let loose. I jokingly told her to let the wild hair run free, as though we were talking about a caged mustang yearning to roam freely outside the stables. She would usually laugh and change the subject but eventually she arrived at our social events with her long, ginger hair blowing in the wind like a flourishing flame. She looked like a literal goddess, and her bright, flawless smile was the cherry on top of the living masterpiece that would soon become my wife.

It wasn't until we were in our late twenties when I called her up with the bold intentions of asking her out. She sounded surprised at first, probably at how long it took for me to ask her out, but she gladly accepted. We dated for over a year before I popped the question, to which she also gladly accepted. Then came the ring shopping, the church calling, followed by the five hour ceremony on the hill by the dazzling lake with a glorious sunset to make the scene worthwhile. After we ended the holy matrimony with a long, passionate kiss, we were then called husband and wife before our Lord and the rest of the world.

The fantasy began to fade only a couple years afterward. It began with the doctor's visit. Charlotte was struggling getting out of bed most mornings and would complain about a nagging pain in her joints, legs and arms. Then she started coming home from work with bruises on her arms and hands. At first I was furious, ready to drive to her job and strangle whoever was beating my wife. Sometimes, Charlotte wouldn't notice them until I pointed them out, as though she went through the entire work day without even realizing the strange dark blue marks on her skin. Whenever I asked for an explanation, she would swear that she didn't have a clue where the bruises or the pains were coming from, so we decided to pay the doctor a visit.

I still remembered the grim expression the doctor wore on his aged face when he explained that Charlotte was diagnosed with leukemia. The news stunned all of us. We were only in our early thirties, so diseases like that wouldn't be expected or even be considered a possibility until decades later. The doctor empathized with us as he tried to explain how the symptoms of the disease included bone pains and how it weakened her body so much that it was prone to bruising and bleeding even without rough physical contact. From what we could understand, by the time we'd identified the disease, it had already done a lot of damage to her body. She has already lost half of her body weight; her vibrant, muscle-toned body had morphed into a frail, sickly pale shell of what she once was. The disease had taken so much from her that the treatment and medication prescribed to her barely made a difference.

I remembered how she looked in the hospital bed with half-closed eyes as she weakly looked up at me. Her blue eyes were full of tears and the brilliance they once held had dulled after days of pain. Her beautiful, long red hair was long gone; she lay in the bed with a completely shaven head. She felt embarrassed at first so she wore a bouffant cap over her head most of the time, especially when she had visitors. If it wasn't for her sweet voice, I probably wouldn't have recognized her. I remembered the sensation from her weak hand as she held it against my cheek when she spoke to me.

"We're going to get through this. I'm not going anywhere, Raymond. I love you so, so much," she said as we looked into each other's eyes. My tears fell and soaked in between her thin fingers as she held my cheek, but I didn't dare to look away, partially knowing that that was possibly one of our last moments together.

I received a call from one of the head doctors at the hospital. I knew what to expect when I recognized the caller ID. My worst expectations were proven when he explained what happened.

"Charlotte has passed," he said, trying to sound as sympathetic as any doctor could. I remembered clearing my throat before I told him I was on my way, then sobbing after I hung up the phone. I drove back to Charlotte's room at the hospital, and my heart nearly dropped when I saw her body lay lifeless in the bed. Her parents were there before I showed up and they were already broken down in sobs. My brother, Edward, came over shortly after and hugged me after I explained to him what happened.

The funeral was about a month later. I stared at the veneer casket that was lowered into the earth as dozens of people dressed in black shed tears and held their heads down in respect. I spoke to no one during the entire service, not to Charlotte's parents or mine. Edward was the only one there who basically stood by my side during the entire service, occasionally grasping onto my shoulder with one hand and asking how I was holding up. Of course, I would lie and say I was fine. He knew I was lying, so he stood close by, probably hoping his presence would hinder me from breaking down in front of all those people. Honestly, my soul and body felt too numb to let out any outbursts.

Every night after I left the hospital was spent alone with heartache and guilt. It may not make sense to some, but I still felt the guilt for not doing SOMETHING to save my wife. Over the months, I'd accepted the possibility that we probably did everything we could to battle the leukemia, or at least as much as our insurance would cover. The only thing that I could imagine would change the outcome would be the timing of it all. Maybe if we noticed the symptoms earlier and acted sooner, there could've been a chance that–

"Raymond? Raymond?" A voice snapped me out of a trance. I quickly withdrew my stare at the squares of gray drywall on the ceiling and returned my attention to my therapist, Madeline, who sat adjacent to me and the recliner I laid on. The middle-aged woman with black and partially silver hair tapped her pen on her notepad as she looked at me. "Raymond, I need you here," she said.

"I-I am," I stammered, realizing I nearly forgot where I was.

"I need you here *mentally*, Raymond. Now back to the question I asked. Have you thought about what we discussed last week?"

I nodded, even though I hadn't a clue what we'd discussed last week. "Good. Then what hobby did you decide to look into?" she asked intently, looking for an answer.

I exhaled and said, "Well, I was looking into this fishing club that I heard about recently. I just didn't find the time because of work and all."

Madeline nodded and scribbled something on her little notepad with a raised eyebrow as though she didn't believe me. She wouldn't be wrong if she didn't. If I was honest, I would tell her that I hadn't been looking for any hobbies or activities that could distract me from my grief. In fact, I'd grown accustomed to it the past year since Charlotte died. It was like drowning in sorrow and pain to the point that it evolved into a void, an endless pit littered with guilt and loneliness that I grew addicted to.

I wish I could say my meetings with Madeline were productive, but at this point, they were just an excuse to get out of the house. Before I started going, I was against the idea of visiting a professional stranger with a notepad and a bullshit degree just to express my private feelings and problems with them. Looking back, it was my brother, Edward, who convinced me to go there in the first place. The only takeaway I got was the same message my brother, my parents and the rest of the goddamn world had for me: Move on. Sounded like simple and profound advice, but was just impossible for me to do. I guess it was one of those "better said than done" sort of things.

I left Madeline's office after hearing her give me a speech about looking for a new activity to help me move on and reconnect with myself. Just like before, I told her that I would do just that before leaving and cursing myself for signing up for those bullshit sessions.

I found myself staring into the nothingness as I drove home. I probably ran a red light or two because I was so distracted by my miserable thoughts. For a while now, I would find my mind drifting away from reality. I would remain in this state until I pulled into the driveway. Then I would drag myself out of the car and into the house to end the day.

While I lay in bed, all I could think about was the beautiful, pearly white smile that Charlotte had. I imagined her materializing next to me and turning to me with her beautiful smile. My forced hallucinations wouldn't hold for long, and my visions would retreat, leaving behind an empty space in my bed.

I kept our room the same even after she passed. I kept the same bed which we slept in and I kept photos of her in frames which I dusted daily. Even the dresser where I kept her old clothes still sat near the window. On top of the dresser sat a small rose gold watch that I gifted Charlotte years ago. The watch stopped ticking weeks ago, but I never dared to move it from that spot. The thought of moving it felt…wrong.

On most nights I found it difficult to go to sleep. The eight hour rest that Madeline recommended sounded far-fetched at this point and melatonin pills were not helping anymore. So, on the most difficult nights, I found myself searching the web for ways to overcome depression and grief over a loved one, even though I couldn't find any confidence to actually go through with any of the suggestions, whether it was finding new hobbies, religions, social groups or sports.

I would spend the nights looking up ASMR videos or audiobooks. Eventually I found myself looking up stories and online forums about fictional topics and fandom. That was how I came across stories about urban legends and tales of places and creatures that people debated whether they were real or not. Those readings and audios led me to the rumors of ghosts, seance rituals and occult dealings that sounded intriguing and at the same time, taboo. Then I heard about the Gates of Hades.

When I first came across the title, I immediately thought it was part of some Rick Riordan fandom or maybe some *Clash of the Titans* reference. But the more I looked into it and the more comments I read about the topic, I found that despite the name, it seemed to be a real place. From what I could gather, the Gates of Hades was just as you would think it was. Somewhere out there, in a more ancient and forgotten part of the world, there is a pathway that leads to the realm of the dead, or "the underworld." Now I wasn't sure if this was the same underworld that was mentioned in *The Odyssey*. There weren't any comments suggesting that. There were, however, rumors that the Gates served as a direct link to meet and communicate with the dead.

At this point you can kinda get the idea of where this story is going, but can you really blame me? I mean, there I was, struggling to proceed with life after the death of my wife. Loneliness, guilt and sorrow were the only things on my mind. Therefore, when I first heard about the Gates of Hades and what they could do, I felt an unexplainable desire to learn more.

At first, everything about it seemed based completely on Greek mythology and fairy tales. After leaving questions in some of the online forums, I found that people actually went there. From what I gathered, there were almost a dozen people who actually went to the actual Gates of Hades, but when I tried asking for those people's contact info, no one seemed to have it. In fact, most of the forums said that most of the people who visited the gates, either NEVER returned to the world of the living or, if they did, they came back "mentally impaired" or basically bat-shit crazy.

One of the forums told me that a woman from New Jersey took a trip to the Gates and returned home. When she returned, she stopped showing up to work and immediately stopped using any form of social media. One day, when the landlord came to check on her at her apartment, he called the police to report a dead body. When the cops arrived, they found a bloated corpse hanging from the ceiling fan in the center of the apartment by a cable cord.

None of her friends or close relatives knew why she decided to take her life so suddenly, but many people in the online community inferred that she had been acting distant and strange since her return from the Gates.

At this point, I decided that the only two negative outcomes I could expect from all of this would be to become clinically insane (which I was certainly on the verge of anyway) or to never find the so-called Gates of Hades. The search for more information ended when I received a chat request from an anonymous user. I decided to read their comment and saw their name was *Gallow$84*. At first, I didn't take the user seriously when they contacted me, especially since their username was spelled "gallows" with a dollar sign, but when they DMed me, I was shocked when I started to read their message.

Hello. I see you're looking for more info on the Gates of Hades. Well, let me save you the trouble by telling you you are not gonna find any real intel here or anywhere online. And don't bother going onto those dark websites. You won't find anything there either. Trust me, I've checked. But if you really want to get details on what you're getting yourself into, then I'm your guy.

At the end of the message was a smiling face emoji. A yellow face grinning at me somehow gave me a chill but it didn't stop me from responding. I figured if this guy was pulling a prank or running some scammer ad, it wouldn't take long to find out. I replied to the person with this:

Lol. And what makes you the expert on the Gates of Hades? Do I have to subscribe to one of your tutorials on YouTube first?

I immediately lost interest, so I clicked off the chat room and shut my computer down to prepare for bed. I wasn't in the mood for dealing with online trolls and scam artists. But a second later, my laptop chimed. I returned to the chat room and found that Gallow$84 had responded. He left another chat bubble:

I understand your skepticism and you'd be right to be so. But I know the reason you want to see the Gates. You've lost someone recently and you want to see them again, don't you?

I stared at the computer screen for a while. Not once since I'd been communicating with people on the forums have I mentioned anything about losing a loved one. I'd asked my questions as someone who was simply curious about the place would, so I couldn't imagine how this user would draw the conclusion so suddenly.

Before I could respond, another bubble appeared on screen:

Were they a spouse? It often is with you people.

That was when I had to respond. I asked this user what they meant by "you people". A moment later, they sent another message:

I meant the usual people who are drawn to it are mostly widows and widowers. Occasionally, people would go to the Gates just to see their lost loved ones, like children or parents. I had one guy come to me just so they could see their dog. It was a strange request, but we made it happen.

I realized now that this was getting weird. Looking back, I should've stopped talking to this person, but I was too triggered to drop the whole conversation. When I asked what they were talking about and what they were trying to sell to me, they sent a message. This time there was a grainy photo of a cave at the edge of a river. Inside was a row of lanterns aligned across the inside of the opening. It was hard to explain, but I felt a strange energy from the picture. There was an unnerving yet alluring power held within that photo. The user must've known he'd gotten my attention when he replied with a message bubble:

The Gates are REAL. If you truly want to see that person again, I can help you find this place. Just know, it will come with a price.

After reading the last message, I closed the computer shut and went to bed. I just couldn't stand the vagueness of the conversation anymore so I tried to leave the search alone. For days, I ignored the laptop and disregarded any chimes or notifications from any of the forums. This didn't last forever though. It started with a dream I had a few nights later. I found myself staring at the cave from the photo, only this time I was actually there. I stood before the massive mouth of the cave as the flames along the walls continued to dance and flicker. I could hear deep, eerie moans and coarse whispers from inside, as though there were dozens of people calling out to me, but I saw no one inside.

All I could see was darkness at first. A moment later, I heard soft, wet footsteps coming from inside the cave, like bare feet slowly slapping on moist rock. A silhouette appeared, and when my sight adjusted on their legs and their small, feminine form, I instantly recognized her. I felt a jolt of surprise and excitement when I saw Charlotte emerge from the darkness but the feeling was replaced by confusion. Then the confusion was replaced by fear as she walked closer to me.

At first, I thought she looked the same as before, yet the closer she got, the less "human" she seemed. She was an entity posing as my wife; a walking, possibly sentient puzzle with obvious missing pieces. Her eyes were absent, leaving her eye sockets completely empty, but that didn't stop her from leaving her eyelids wide open as if trying to use her nonexistent eyeballs. Her mouth was a gaping maw and her jaws looked to be crooked, as if the top and bottom were pulled in opposing directions. Her hair that was once lively and fiery was no longer ginger-colored. It was now a dull brown with bald patches scattered across her scalp. Her skin was sickly pale and barely hanging onto her bones.

I froze in terror and confusion as this thing poorly masqueraded as my wife continued to approach me. When she finally stopped, she was only a foot away. Her empty eye sockets aimed at my face as though she could still see me, and her crooked jaws began to shift and crack as she tried to talk.

A rough, dry voice forced its way through the entity's throat and whispered,"Raymond? Where are you? Where are you?"

I immediately woke up after that. My back and neck were slick with sweat as I jolted upright in the bed. I felt myself still shaking as I started breathing heavily. For a while, I sat in the center of the bed, the same bed that me and Charlotte shared only a year ago. I took a glance at the side of the bed where she would've slept if she was still alive. Then my eyes glossed around the room and looked at her dresser and the rose gold watch that sat on the shelf. I got out of bed and started moving through the drawers. Her old shirts, jeans and pajamas were still neatly folded in there. I picked up some of the clothing, brought them close to my face and took a deep whiff. Her scent was on them, but much fainter now after not being worn for so long.

It was at that moment that I realized that moving on was such a Herculean task for me because I didn't want to. I refused to leave the past where it belonged and accept that Charlotte's death was something I actually had to make peace with. I refused to accept it, and the pain, sorrow and nightmares were the demons governing the perpetual hell I was confined in. I figured there was only one way to escape it.

I waited until I got back from work the following day before I got on the computer. I went back to the one-on-one group chat where I messaged Gallow$84 and saw that they had messaged me while I was at work. They asked me if I wanted to end the conversation and said that they'd just go to someone else who'll be grateful for what they had to offer. I reluctantly typed back, asking them to tell me everything I needed to know.

Just as soon as I clicked ENTER, I saw an icon on Gallow$84's side of the chatroom indicating that they were already typing. A long minute passed as I sat on the edge of my seat. I was so eager for a response that I felt the hairs on my arms and neck stand up. My room was so silent, I could only hear my clock ticking away near my bed stand, and the sound of my laptop chiming after the user finally responded. This time, they sent a paragraph. When I began to read it, I realized it was instructions that included an address and a time to meet, and they were explicit about me coming alone.

The user then explained that the things they needed to tell me could not be said online. They told me it would get the attention of the "wrong people."

I would be lying if I said that I wasn't skeptical and didn't have any second thoughts about all this. My heart felt like it was falling into the pit of my stomach as I read the instructions. The specifics they provided were alarming enough, everything from the time to meet and the place we had to go to WHERE to sit at the location and which direction to face until they arrived. The most unnerving part about all of it was that the location was just down the street from me. I didn't recall giving out my personal info to anyone, so I was perplexed on how this person—he or she or a robot or whatever—just so happened to choose a place that was not only in my city and state, but in my neighborhood. I suddenly felt like I was being watched, but that didn't stop me from replying to Gallow$84 that I would comply with the instructions. They replied with a thumbs-up emoji.

I drove toward the address Gallow$84 had instructed. It was a small coffee shop that was about ten minutes down my street. I was greeted by the smell of freshly made donuts and fritters that the employees placed on display for the morning rush. A long line of people extended from the front door to the counter where a group of baristas were rushing to take orders. I wanted to get a cup of coffee for myself and I thought about getting one for my mysterious online friend. Then I decided it would be best to find my seat and get this meeting over with.

The message I read the night before told me to take a seat toward the rear of the cafe where two booths were placed against each other. I made my way past the busy crowd of people until I found the booths. To my surprise, there was one empty booth in front of another. In the second booth sat a figure with a dark gray hoodie. As I slowly approached, I shot brief glances at the person to see their face. But all I could see was a dark hoodie pulled over their face, completely concealing it in a shadow. The hoodie was long-sleeved and their cargo pants and tall black boots covered every inch of skin. I looked at their hands and realized even they were covered. The person wore beige vinyl gloves and laced their fingers while they sat patiently.

I felt on edge as I sat down behind them, still unsure if they saw me or not. I slightly looked at the figure from my peripheral.

"PavedWay42," the hooded man whispered to me

Immediately I drew my attention away from the person after they spoke. They had a deep, cold masculine tone of voice that struck me like razor-sharp icicles falling from a rooftop. I asked carefully, "Uh what?"

"Are you PavedWay42?" the person asked. It took me a moment to compute, but then I remembered that PavedWay42 was my online username.

I replied,"Yes, that's me. Are you Gal–"

"Not here," the person snapped, immediately silencing me and reminding me that this was a discreet and secret interaction. "And yes, I'm him. Now before we continue, I need to know something. Who came here with you?"

"Nobody. I drove alone," I said.

"Were you followed?"

"I-I, uh…I don't think so. Why would I be followed?"

"Let's just say these subjects aren't meant to be discussed between regular folk."

I kept facing ahead as Gallow$84 spoke behind me. I looked around at the other people in the cafe. I carefully and quickly looked at the baristas, the hippies with skateboards, and the businessmen and lawyers that talked with each other as we sat. I wondered to myself if there were any FBI agents or cops sitting in this cafe listening to me as I talked to this weirdo.

"So you still want to learn about how to get to the Gates?"

"Uh…well, yes," I slowly said, still unsure about anything I was doing at this point.

"How much do you know?"

I sat for a moment to recall what I'd already learned about the Gates. As I did, I saw flashes of the nightmare I had a couple nights ago and remembered why I was here. This place, wherever it is, was calling me. I couldn't explain it, but I had a feeling that the dream was more of an omen or a foreshadowing of what was going to happen, and it had something to do with that cave which I knew had to be the Gates of Hades.

"I've heard that it's a real place," I said. "Everyone who knows about it says that you can meet with the lost souls."

"And I take it there is someone you want to meet?" Gallow$84 asked this as though he already knew the answer.

"My wife, Charlotte," I answered.

"Ah. Of course."

"What do you mean 'of course'?"

"It's the Gates. It's luring you to it by now, probably. It takes an interest in those who lost a loved one, especially those who are cursed with grief and pain. It probably thinks you're a worthy candidate. Let me guess, you've already started having dreams, haven't you?"

I sat in silence trying to understand what I just heard. First off, why did he talk about the Gates of Hades as if it sought people like a predator? And how did he know about my dreams? When I realized I'd been silent for too long, I simply replied with a meek,"Yeah."

I heard the hooded man lean back in his seat and give a deep and tired sigh. "Well, you were right about one thing. The place is real. And although you can communicate with the dead there, most people don't. There are certain *requirements* you need in order to survive that far."

"Survive?" I asked.

"Of course. Surely you know most people don't even come back from this place. Even the ones who do are fucked up in one way or another. Or they just disappear. Now just so you know, this place isn't exactly hell. All it is is a doorway to the afterlife."

"If it's not hell, then what afterlife does it lead to?"

Gallow$84 thought for a moment before saying, "I don't know actually. Everyone has a different experience. You know, the funny thing about people is that we have worshiped countless gods and made so many religions, nearly all of them having their own idea of what the afterlife would look like. I guess that's the secret behind it all. Maybe whatever version of the afterlife the soul goes to depends on what they believe. Or maybe it's up to the universe or God to decide what they're worthy of. I don't have a clue about any of that shit though. I'm a collector and an adventurer in a sense, not a preacher."

After hearing this, I saw a folded paper dangling in front of my face tauntingly. "Take it," Gallow$84 said. I took the paper and opened it to find that it was a regular world map with highlighter marks on it. I followed the tracings along a riverway in the western part of Greece. Along the tracings were other markings and checkmarks which I figured were checkpoints or rest areas or something.

"So the Gate of Hades is in Greece?"

"Shocking, isn't it? It shouldn't be a huge surprise but there were once other ways to the Gates. You see, the Gates aren't exactly in Greece, but one of the rivers in the country can take you there. There are five rivers in the world that can take you to one of the Gates, according to the tales. From what I've found, most of the rivers either just don't exist or are too risky for a normal human to ride down. The River Styx is a well-known one, but the others were Cocytus, Lethes, Phlegethon and Acheron. Trust me, you don't want to use Styx or Lethes and you damn sure won't survive Phlegathon. I don't know anyone who found Cocytus. So your best bet is the Acheron, which runs in the western region of the country. Still though, it's gonna cost you."

It always comes down to money, I thought. I should have expected this guy would want a money bag from me eventually. "How much?" I asked. I was ready to sum all of this up to be a lame scam before he held a Velcro strap over my head. I looked close at the strap and noticed that it had a camera connected to the center. It was some sort of head strap with a small camera lens connected to a small black box that I'd seen bikers and rock climbers wear to record their travels.

I slowly took it to examine it and Gallow$84 said,"Like I said, I'm an adventurer, but even a trip to the afterlife is where I draw the line. Believe me, I would *kill* to see the Gates myself. But I've always been a solitary person. The Gates would never call to me because I don't have family or friends or any spouse. The only thing death can take from me is me. But you, well, I've helped people like you many times. You have someone in the afterlife you want to talk to. Now, what you say to them when you get there is none of my business, but since you are the type of person the Gate would want, you'll be perfect to help me with my research."

Finally, I started to understand what I was getting into. "So let me get this straight. You want me to help you by recording my trip to the Gates for your research?"

"Seems fair to me. You want to see your wife again. I'm helping you to do that. I've tried going myself once, but the Gates never revealed themselves because the Acheron River will only transport you there if the Gates want you to see it. And the only way to be chosen is to have someone in mind you desperately want to see and some considerable amount of emotional baggage from their death. It sorta feeds off that type of shit, you know? I just need you to record everything you see. I've done this with many others before, and each time I pay for the round trip and the boat. All you gotta do is survive."

I listened to Gallow$84's spiel, knowing any sane man would've walked away long ago. I wasn't, unfortunately. But at this point, I had nothing else to lose. What difference would a free trip to some river in western Greece make to my miserable life? At least I could add it to my bucket list. Another reason I was sold on the idea was because I knew the place was real. I'd seen the Gates in my dream and my wife was there waiting to see me. I just knew it.

After talking, Gallow$84 reached behind himself to hand me a few more items: a notepad with a bunch of words scribbled on it, a dirty coin that took up half the palm of my hand, a large tape recorder and a plane ticket to Greece. He then told me to take the flight and rent a row-boat to take to the river. He said to wait until nightfall, place the coin on the front of the boat and read the words on the notepad outloud. He also told me to bring something that belonged to the deceased person I wanted to communicate with, which I decided would be the rose gold watch Charlotte used to wear.

He then told me to not argue with the "ferryman," to which I shrugged and said, "Okay." He went on to tell me what to do when I reached the Gate of Hades, which involved the tape recorder he gave me, but I'll get to that later.

A week later, my flight landed in Greece. The Gallow guy gave me the ticket for free and when I looked up the average price for the same trip, I found it was almost two grand. A part of me questioned what kind of "collector" or "adventurer" had that kind of money to throw away so willingly. Then again, if this trip was just a journey to prove to the world that the Gates of Hades existed and all I had to do was help some mysterious hooded man in a coffee shop get some footage in exchange for a free trip, then I was down.

After getting a few modes of transportation, I found my way to the southwest region near the Acheron. There, I found a small boat shop based on an address Gallow$84 gave me. It was a small shack that stood in front of a yard full of boats. I saw yachts, sail boats and a dozen row boats that looked to be in my price range. After looking around for the shop owner and checking through the inventory for a cheap yet sturdy boat, we were able to agree on a white wooden row-boat around twelve feet long. I told the owner I only needed it for one full day, which would allow me to use it that night— probably the most unnerving aspect of this entire trip.

Later that night, I brought my camping gear, Charlotte's watch and the items that Gallow$84 gave me onto the boat before pushing it into the river. The sun was setting by then, leaving a sliver of gold in the sky and the clouds were transforming from the light purple haze into a dark blue. I remembered asking Gallow$84 why this voyage had to take place at night. According to him, there was a ferryman that would lead me to the Gates, but he was only available at night. When he told me this, I assumed there was a local guide or ranger who might be on duty around this time. Then I figured since this trip was supposed to be some sort of secret mission, the "ferryman" was probably a friend of his.

When I started paddling down the stream, I took in the sight of the evening atmosphere. I admired the tall rocky slopes that towered over the river, the birds that called to each other as the sun lowered itself at the horizon and the dancing trees that seemed to greet me as I continued down the river. When the darkness started to take hold of my surroundings, I took out my LED torch light, set it in front of me, and placed the head strap and camera on my head. I pushed the button on the side to make sure it was recording, otherwise this trip would be a waste of time. I paddled onward into the approaching night.

Just as Instructed, when there was no source of light other than my LED torch, I reached into my backpack for the old coin. I looked at it for a moment, wondering if I saw a few fragments of gold underneath the grime that coated it. I reached toward the front of the boat and placed it on the bow. I took out the notebook and began to read the words in it outloud.

"I, Raymond, am requesting passage to the world beyond life. I ask permission from Aides, the Unseen, the Invisible One, He Who Grants Wealth, The Governor of the Lost Souls, the Director to the Land of Fire and Wheat Fields…"

The script went on and on like some sort of prayer to whom I figured was supposed to be Hades from the ancient Greek religion, although I read a few parts calling him by his Roman name, Pluto. There were even some parts written with English letters but with words that clearly weren't in any English dictionary. As I struggled to pronounce them, they almost sounded like the Greek languages that the locals spoke, though some of it sounded Latin.

After I was done reading the words out loud, the torch light flickered for a moment. I looked around, only to find shadows of the crooked tree branches that dipped into the dark, murky waters that carried me. Everything was quiet, as though the world was set on mute. I started feeling a sense of terror creep over me when I thought I heard a whooshing sound behind me. When I looked, I saw nothing but pitch-blackness, but when I turned a second time, I nearly fell backward in the boat and whipped out my switchblade at what stood in front of me.

It was a person…sort of. They had the shape of a hunched, elderly man with dark and muddy tattered clothing and tall boots. I felt my heart beat at top speed and stared in horror as I tried to see his face. He didn't have one. The LED light that sat between us only illuminated the filthy clothes and the fisherman hat. Underneath the hat was a dark cloudy mass, indiscernible except for a pair of glowing white, almost milky eyes that reflected in the light.

I spoke, trying to sound authoritative but only ended up trembling and stuttering as I questioned the specter. "Wh-Who are you? How did you get here?"

The shadowy being cocked his head to the side and ignored me as he bent over to pick up the coin which I'd placed down earlier. He brought it close to his pupil-less, cloudy eyes to examine it. I saw the ghostly eyes blink and turn toward me. A moment later, he pocketed the coin and I heard a low, raspy voice come from the shadowy nothingness under the figure's hat.

"You seek the Gates?" the being said slowly.

I nodded and nearly flinched when the being turned and faced the bow of the boat. Suddenly, the boat began to change course and turn down one of the perpendicular streams of the river. The paddles remained inside the boat as they pushed themselves through the water with some unseen force. I had no doubt that the shadow dressed as a fisherman was doing all of this. I remembered hearing the stories about Greek heroes who traveled to the underworld and had to meet Charon, a ferryman who patrolled the waters of the River Styx. If this was the same ancient Greek deity from the stories, then that would mean he was leading me to the actual Gates of Hades.

The boat veered down another stream, only this one looked murkier than the rest of the tributaries, almost stagnant. I noticed that the farther the boat went, I could no longer see shadows of the trees and bushes on the edge of the riverbank. In fact, I could barely see land at all. What I was able to see was a thick mist that shrouded the edge of the river. I looked at the map of the river system and I couldn't recognize this part at all. It almost looked as if the world had vanished into a long endless, dark and filthy water-way surrounded by a vast and ominous body of mist. The ferryman, however, didn't seem bothered by this as he continued looking onward from the bow, somehow guiding my boat with some supernatural force that I had no business witnessing.

Something caught my attention from the corner of my eye, causing me to look over the edge of the boat. The water was now so dark that it looked black, even darker than the night sky that was supposed to reflect off it. I saw no signs of life under its surface. No fish, no crustaceans, not even a leaf from the trees. But I *did* see something moving through it. A large bubble emerged from the black water like a translucent wart or tumor actively forcing itself out of a layer of gooey membrane. Then the bubble popped, releasing a gust of a soot-colored vapor. I tried to cover my nose when the vapor blew toward my face but I was too late. The odor wasn't toxic but it did have a raw, putrid scent that reminded me of a foul combination of rotted roadkill and sulfur.

I gagged and coughed heavily after smelling the disgusting odor from the water, confused after realizing that the water smelled nothing close to this an hour ago. I pushed myself to the center of the boat to recover and got a panoramic view of the river. All around us were more bubbles that oozed and exploded into gross vapor. The water looked like a pitch-black jacuzzi with filth and mist surrounding it.

The ferryman called to me while still facing the front of the boat and said,"Stay clear from the waters. The river is alive and it will devour anyone who touches its water or inhales its fumes."

I took heed and did just as the Ferryman commanded. But even as I stayed away from the water, I felt something take hold of me. It was like a wave had rushed over my soul, leaving me with a dull and heavy sadness. The sadness and loneliness I'd endured for months after Charlotte died was NOTHING compared to the emptiness and sorrow that now gnawed at my soul. Somehow I knew this was the river working some sort of power over me.

The sadness came almost out of nowhere and had no reason to be activated. Yes, I was still grieving for my beloved Charlotte but the thoughts I had of her passing never provoked the feelings I felt while riding across that river. The heavy melancholy was powerful, making me feel like the most microscopic and pitiful thing in all of creation. For that entire time, I forgot that any other sensation or emotion even existed. Fear, hate, love, indifference, joy, anger, lust, even rage were all foreign concepts. The only thing I felt while I sat on that boat was sadness and sorrow that continued to latch on and gnaw at my very being. It was so sickening that I found myself falling over and coiling into a fetal position.

Tears ran down my cheeks nonstop as I wailed and screamed like a dying animal. It was then that I realized the ferryman meant when he said the river was alive. It was a parasite; it was leeching onto my mind and my soul, draining any emotion and anything that made me human.

"It-It's gonna kill me," I sobbed, nearly choking on my own tears and mucus. "It's killing me."

"Death takes all things," said the ferryman with an indifference in his tone. "Especially in this part of reality. The River of Woe is doing what it has done for thousands of years. It is only taunting you. It is up to you to resist its hold. I cannot help you or interfere."

At first I didn't understand what he was saying, but I felt a creeping realization forced into my head from somewhere else. This was too familiar for me not to know what was happening. It was the feeling of defeat and the creeping desire to end my own suffering.

I screamed out loud, "No! You can't have me! I won't let you." Instinctively I reached into my backpack and pulled out some rope I used to tie knots on camping trips. I immediately placed my legs together and tied my ankles to the seat in the boat. Then I lay there, still holding my head as the river continued putting self-destructive thoughts and emotions in my mind.

By then, I was feeling as though I was wasting time. The defeatist desire to end the pain and suffering was at its peak. My eyes kept drifting to the edge of the boat where the black water continued to bubble and hiss. I felt a powerful urge to hurl myself over the edge, knowing the gruesome outcome that would follow. I felt my legs act on their own, trying to wriggle out of the bindings I put them in. I now had no control over myself; my entire body was sliding and pushing itself away from the ropes that kept me tied to the boat. The whole time I groaned and screamed at the river, my body, and the dark forces that were forcing me to want to die.

A few minutes later, the feeling subsided and my body felt free from whatever force had been pulling me toward that foul river. I felt as though I had control again. The ferryman turned and came down from the bow and glared at me with a ghostly stare.

"We are here," he growled.

I sat up to look over the edge of the boat and found that we'd drifted onto a rocky beach. Beyond the rocky beach stood a massive stone wall that towered before us. My eyes bulged when I saw the large cave that appeared through the retreating mist. It looked exactly as I remembered from my dream; the lit torches that were set up inside the mouth had flames that danced in the darkness. I couldn't see or hear anything from the cave, but continued to cut through the rope around my ankles and brought my backpack and gear with me as I exited the boat.

The ferryman looked down at me as I prepared to continue my journey. When my shoes touched the rocky surface of the beach, I heard a whooshing sound behind me. When I turned, there was no sign of the ferryman. It was as though he vanished into thin air, or he was never there at all. I didn't ponder where he went for too long and I walked up the beach and toward the Gates of Hades.

I stopped walking as I made it to the edge of the cave. I squinted into the darkness but saw nothing but the fires flickering along the walls. I turned on my LED torch light and aimed it into the cave. It looked like it was an endless tunnel that led to nothing but more pitch-blackness.

At this point, I remembered one of Gallow$84's final instructions which involved the tape recorder. According to him, the tape had a recording that must be played upon entering the cave. When I asked him why, he said it was crucial and would save my life when I met the guard.

Now, I probably didn't heed this instruction as I should have. I was filled with so much astonishment and trepidation that I forgot the instruction and started to proceed into the cave like a wandering tourist. I had the tape with me but it was still in my backpack. I decided to walk deeper into the cave with soft footsteps and focused on making myself as light and quiet as possible. Apparently my stealth needed improvement, because I was barely ten feet into the cave when I heard something heavy stirring ahead. First I heard a heavy thud followed by the sound of something sharp scraping the hard ground ahead. Then I heard something sniffing the air vigorously.

I completely froze in place. I started to back away slowly without making too much noise but by then it was too late. The thing that was resting at the end of the tunnel was approaching me, and I was finally able to see that the creature was large, judging by the shadow. My terror forced me to back away outside of the cave, and the creature was now emerging from the tunnel into the moonlight, which was when I fell back in horror.

The first thing I saw were three large animals staring down at me. As they snarled and crept closer to me, I saw that the three animals' heads were all conjoined at the same neck. The body of the creature looked like it belonged to a massive, muscular predator. The dark fur was matted and its four legs had paws with wickedly long, dagger-like claws that scraped the ground as they walked. The three heads were the most bizarre and unbelievably terrifying aspect of the beast. The head in the center belonged to a large gray wolf, and it snapped its jaws at me with rage flickering in its blood-red eyes. The head on the left side belonged to a greyhound that had foam dripping from its mouth and the head on the right belonged to a hyena that growled and cackled as it sniffed at me.

All three heads glared down at me with their fangs bared and an aura of fury radiating from their eyes. I knew I had to act but with the corruptive river behind me and a three-headed monstrosity in front of me, I didn't know what to do. I reached into my pocket for my switchblade, aimed the knife at the heads, and swung it in the air. That was my worst mistake. The creature reared back, completely dodging the blade, and then with one swipe of its large claws, it tossed me aside like a bowling pin.

I landed on the ground with a rough thud that nearly knocked all the wind from my chest. I groaned and looked down at my body and saw a large set of gashes from the terrible claws that raked across the side of my stomach. I noticed my backpack had been knocked away from me and some of my gear had scattered on the ground. There was the rope I used earlier, Charlotte's watch, and the tape. The beast never moved any of its eyes from me, and had begun to slowly approach. I knew from how both the greyhound and the wolf heads licked their chops and the hyena head hooted and cackled, it was clear that the monster was intending to finish me off.

I then reached for the tape, Gallow$84's words echoing in my head, and strained my sore and scraped arm to press the small play button on the side of the device. A second later the tape made a clicking sound and began to play a song. It was a harmonious melody with feminine vocals. It was like listening to a siren with a whimsical and alluring voice that almost sounded like a lullaby.

"Are you fucking kidding me?" I yelled at the tape, thinking that this was some kind of joke or a prank that was gonna get me ripped to pieces. But then I stopped to listen and realized the beast's footsteps stopped. When I looked up, I was stunned to see the monster was…calm.

The creature was looking at the tape player as the music played and its three heads began to sway in a sleepy motion. I realized that the tape was having a hypnotic effect that was distracting it. *This is why he wanted me to play the tape before I went into the cave,* I thought to myself.

I wasted no time. I gathered my backpack and ran from the beast while it was infatuated with the tape player. Just when I was about to reenter the cave, I stopped and cursed at myself when I realized I'd left Charlotte's watch on the ground. According to Gallow$84, that watch was the only way I would be able to find Charlotte in the world of the dead. I took a quick glance at the monster to make sure it was still distracted. When I saw it was looking more drowsy than before, I bolted to where I lay recently. I frantically searched the ground for the watch. Luckily, I found it. The moonlight glistened on the face of the watch as I looked at it.

I was certain my journey was to be finally completed when something caught my attention. I turned when I heard the tape start skipping. I noticed that half of the tape was dented and cracked from when it was knocked out of my bag. It continued to pause and skip until the lullaby turned into a slow mechanical voice that was badly distorted. The beast immediately noticed the song was interrupted and snapped back into focus. It turned to me and all three of its heads wore a furious expression before it started running at me with full speed.

I turned to sprint into the cave. I pushed and gasped for air as I forced my body to run, but the heavy panting and the wet snarls only came closer and closer behind me. I was barely a foot into the cave when a wall of force knocked me again. This time, the blow slammed me against the wall. I slid down pitifully onto my back and groaned in agony. A moment later I felt the beast's paw slam onto my chest and it held me in place like a cat holding down a mouse. The paw was big enough that it covered my shoulders and my chest. One of the claws nearly touched my neck as the three heads peered down at me, jaws wide open and ready to devour me.

I'm not sure why I did what I did next, but it probably saved my life. I held up the watch tightly in my hand and held it between me and the monster's center head which was closest to me. Tears began streaming down my face as I understood that my journey was going to end with me becoming food to some three-headed demon. However, I still held the watch in the air. This was the piece of Charlotte I'd brought with me and it may have been the last thing I touched before I died. I looked at the three terrifying heads and muttered,"Charlotte. Charlotte. If you are in this cave, just know that I love you. Just know I've tried."

Suddenly, the wolf head closed its mouth, as if processing what I just said. Then the greyhound closed its jaws, followed by the hyena. They all drew their attention to the watch in my hand. The hyena head brought its nose close to get a sniff of the watch and made a squealing sound. Then it looked at the other two heads. They traded glances for a moment and then returned their gaze down on me. To my horror, the wolf head opened its jaws wide. Its sharp teeth glistened with saliva and its breath smelled like a dozen rotten carcasses.

I closed my eyes and waited for the monster's teeth to close around my flesh. But I felt nothing. I opened my eyes slowly and was shocked to see a blue glow flicker from inside the wolf's throat. I looked at the glowing light, expecting something terrible to happen. Instead, I heard a voice calling out to me. It was a feminine voice and it sounded confused and just as shocked as I was.

"Raymond," the voice said almost singingly. I didn't respond because I was still confused with what I was seeing and hearing. "Raymond. Can you hear me?"

It can't be, I thought. I shed a final tear as my eyes widened in shock. "Charlotte?" I asked.

"Yes. Yes, I'm here."

"How is this possible? You can't be. How are you talking to me?" I looked at my hand that was still holding the watch. It was still in one piece without a single crack, even after being tossed around by a three headed hell hound. Then it dawned on me that the beast that was attacking me was none other than Cerberus, the guard dog of the underworld. I noted that it looked nothing like how Disney portrayed it in *Hercules*, but nonetheless I was still perplexed with what I was seeing.

Charlotte's voice responded, "I don't know, Ray. But I miss you so much. You actually found the Gates of Hades? How did you even find out about this place?"

I spoke to the light inside the wolf's throat and gave a brief story of how I found the place, starting from the forums, then the mysterious user, then the trip and the ferryman. Charlotte's voice chuckled as though she couldn't believe what she was hearing. We continued talking for a few moments, trading inside jokes that we'd known since we were younger. For a moment, I felt a surge of joy and nostalgia that I hadn't felt in a long time. It was her. It was really, really her.

"We've known each other since highschool, Ray. I never thought you would be a creepypasta fanatic, let alone an adventurer. Why would you do all of this? Do you know how dangerous this is?"

"I know, but I had to see you, Charlotte. I love you and I just…I just couldn't let you go."

There was a pause in her voice. For a moment I thought I said something wrong, or maybe her spirit or whatever was allowing her voice to be heard had left. Then her voice returned with a regretful sigh.

"This is all because of me," she said shamefully.

"No," I said,"I did all of this FOR you. To be with you again. It was my decision."

"No, Raymond. You don't understand. You're not supposed to be here. Do you know what you're doing? That's why the hellhound won't let you pass. This place isn't for the living. The only way we can actually be together is if you—"

"I know," I cut her off. I always somewhat knew that seeing her would mean that I wasn't gonna be able to come back. I knew that after reading the forums and I was fine with that. "I was so broken after I lost you," I added. "There is nothing left for me here. Don't you understand that?"

Charlotte spoke, this time with a deep sadness in her voice. "Ray. You can't. The Gates won't let you through to the afterlife without consuming you first. You are tampering with forces neither you or I could ever understand."

I snapped, "I don't care about the forces. I don't care about the Gates of Hades or whatever god is in charge of all this. I just want you, Charlotte. I love you so much that I'm willing to die for you."

"You don't have to die for me to love me," she said. "If you love me so much, then don't die for me. Live for me! Continue the life that I couldn't. Go start more adventures like the one you just told me. Make your time in that world worth living so that when your time does come, the right way, then you can tell me everything you've lived through. Can you do that for me?"

I was lost for words. I stared at the light, looking for something to say to argue with Charlotte's spirit, but she was right. About everything. Of course she wouldn't want me to throw my life away, especially not like this. I realized now I was being selfish. I wasn't throwing my life away for her; I was risking my life because I gave up on life. I felt too overwhelmed by the loneliness and sadness that engulfed my mediocre life. Then I recalled what I'd endured when I resisted against the bubbling river. I survived that because the will to go on was still guiding me. I realized that that same will and desire to keep fighting was what I needed to continue with my life in general. To be alive was to be resistant and strong. And that alone, I decided, would be my greatest gift to Charlotte.

I thought for a while and I nodded to her. She must've seen me because she said,"I love you, Ray. But this isn't your time. Not yet. Cerberus can still show you mercy, but you have to tell him that you'll leave and never return."

I hesitated at first, but I mustered the courage and said,"I'll leave. And I promise to never return." My voice trembled and I flinched when the beast started moving again. The wolf's mouth started to shut.

Just before the mouth closed, the blue light flickered once more and Charlotte's voice rang out. "I love you!"

Before I could respond, the light vanished and the wolf's mouth closed. Then it lifted its massive paw from my chest. All three heads were looking down at me now like they were waiting for me to do something. As soon as I stood up, the wound on my side and the pain in my back reminded me of the recent ass-whooping this creature gave me. Then I turned and walked away from the beast and out of the mouth of the cave.

I didn't look back until I knew I was out of the cave. When I did, I saw Cerberus staring back at me. Three heads stared at me, as if it was making sure I wasn't gonna break my promise. I didn't move an inch. After a while, the beast turned and started to walk back into the tunnel until he vanished into the blackness within. A moment later, I felt a hard tremor around me. Suddenly, the rocks from around the cave opening began to shift and crash into each other. Like squares shifting on a colossal Rubik's Cube, the rocks eventually sealed themselves, and the cave was no longer visible.

I didn't recall anything else happening that night. I assumed I passed out or just fell asleep from all the stress and terror I'd witnessed. All I knew was that when I opened my eyes, the first thing I saw was the morning sunrise. When I sat up, I looked around, expecting to be surrounded by bubbling, murderous water, talking shadows and demonic guard dogs. Instead, I saw nothing that reminded me of last night other than the beach, but instead of the rocky conglomerates that I walked on before, I found myself sitting on a river bank covered in silt.

The river wasn't bubbling and didn't give off any horrendous odor. Instead the water gently flowed with the stream and carried a soft layer of foam from the surf. Unlike before, I was able to hear the birds and insects that buzzed and chirped throughout the trees that seemed to have returned. There was no mist and the water had a blue and jade-like tint to it. I almost swore I was teleported to an entirely different place, until I stood up and turned around. Then I saw the tall rocky cliffside towering behind me and immediately recognized the spot where the Gates of Hades had once stood.

I was about to walk close to the wall when I felt a sharp sting from the side of my stomach. I looked down and saw the large claw mark on my skin. It looked like it partially closed up overnight, although my shirt was completely torn through and coated in my blood.

That was the end of my trip to the Gates of Hades. I wish I could say it was easy to return home. It wasn't. The row-boat I rented was still on the river-bank. I spent over an hour yelling for help as I paddled along the stream. The map was no help, since I didn't recall how I got to where I was. Luckily, there were a few bird watchers who heard my cry as they walked alongside the river. They were kind enough to point me in the right direction towards the nearest town. I returned the boat to the shack. After that, I went to the nearest clinic to get my scars cleaned up and stitched, then I went to a local inn to use their Wi-Fi to book a plane ticket home for the following day. Before I rested, I took a look through the camera that was strapped to my head all night. I thought about watching the footage, but I figured I'd check it out later; I was still readjusting after the chaos from the previous night.

Later that evening, I was sitting on the bed watching TV in my room and looking on my phone to decide where my next vacation would be. I figured I'd send Gallow$84 the footage after I returned home since he didn't exactly give a deadline. Hell, he probably assumed I was dead anyway.

My body jolted when I heard a heavy knock at the door. I slowly got up from the bed and walked to the front door. I looked through the peephole and saw no one standing in the hall. I decided to unlock and open the door to get a better look, expecting to see a gang of kids scurrying past. However, as soon as I cracked the door open, something from the otherside slammed into it, forcing me to fall backward into the room. I watched as two men in black suits and shades burst into the room. One of them grabbed me by my shoulders, nearly picking me up from the floor, and forced me into the chair near the corner of the room. The other swiftly closed the door and put the locks on it.

The gravity of the new situation weighed tremendously when I saw myself handcuffed to a chair facing two bald Agent Smith-looking guys glaring down at me like I was America's Most Wanted. I noticed one of them was slightly taller and had a blonde mustache while the other was short and had a potbelly.

"What the hell is this? Who are you? Do you even have a warrant?" I screamed while fighting against my restraints.

The shorter one leaned close enough to me that I could smell the coffee and tobacco on his breath. "Hello. Raymond, is it?"

I said nothing. I noticed the man had an American accent, which was a red flag. Were these guys from the U.S.? Did they follow me this whole time? They obviously knew my name but I decided to keep quiet until I was able to get a lawyer. I began to suspect these were not your usual cops. In fact, I wasn't sure if they were cops at all.

"We know what you did last night, Raymond," the taller agent said with a Southern drawl. "You don't need to play dumb with us."

I looked between the two agents and tried wearing the best clueless expression on my face. "I-I don't have any idea what's going on. Please, I was just on a vacation, that's all–"

I didn't finish my sentence because I was interrupted by a large fist slamming into my left cheek. I felt my head sway quickly and throb after the unforeseen punch from the agent with the potbelly. I sat back up and moved my tongue over my teeth to make sure none of them were knocked out. Luckily, they were all still intact, and my jaw stung, but it didn't feel broken. The short agent crossed his arms and stared at me. His remorseless eyes were distrusting and looked almost predatory, as if he was eager to punch me again. I fucking hated both of these bastards. I'd already made up my mind to sue whatever agency they worked for.

The taller agent smirked as he saw that I'd become flustered. He shifted his stance a little and said, "Listen here, Raymond. You're not in trouble. We're here to ask you a few questions. Now, we already know you found the Gates of Hades. We also can tell by your bandages that you had a scuffle with that hellhound, but seeing that you're alive, you obviously didn't enter the Gates completely. I must say, that's really bold of you. Most people aren't able to resist the effect the Acheron and the Gates have on them. But you pulled through."

I knew the two agents didn't handcuff me to a chair and assault me just to congratulate me for surviving my trip to the Gates. They wanted something else.

"What do you want from me?" I grunted.

"Intel," answered the shorter agent. "Although you're a rare case, you're not the first person to go to Hell and back. And each one of you people have one thing in common: you all got help from the same individual. Tell us what you know about Gallow$84."

A shiver ran up my spine when I heard the name. I knew Gallow$84 was a strange person, but after the trip and the things that he gave me, I knew he wasn't an ordinary man. I sighed and hesitated, then decided I would rather get home and let the CIA or whoever deal with Gallow$84. I told them how I met the guy online and how we met in the coffee shop. I told them I had never seen his face so I couldn't give a description and that seemed to have made both of the agents upset. I then told them about the camera that he told me to wear on my head as I rode the boat to the Gates. That was when both agents looked at me with surprised expressions.

"So he made you take footage of your trip to the Gates? Where is it?" asked the short agent.

I nodded at my backpack that sat on the bed. I knew that if I'd returned home without that footage, I might have trouble when Gallow$84 came looking for it. But at this point, I'd already snitched enough and I was willing to do anything to get these psychos out of my room. The tall agent dug through my bag, tossing out the rope, flashlight, switchblade, and Charlotte's watch.

When he pulled out the camera, he and the short agent huddled together and began tampering with it. Then I heard a video playing from behind me and I recognized the sounds from when I first started traveling on the river. I heard the whooshing sounds from the winds, and the raspy voice from the ferryman that materialized on the boat. I heard the footage fast-forward to when I was screaming and crying while tying myself to the boat to keep from jumping into the evil river. I thought I could hear distinct whispers that I didn't recall hearing the night before. I knew the whispers definitely didn't belong to the ferryman because he was still at the bow by then. Perhaps it was the river whispering to me while simultaneously singing wicked spells into my ears to corrupt me.

The agents fast-forwarded again. This time I could hear the unmistakable snarls and growls from Cerberus as he chased me around the front of the cave. Then I heard the sweet and lovely voice of Charlotte when Cerberus pinned me to the ground. I heard the record end shortly after when the agents shut the camera off. After that there was silence, as if they were trading glances at each other while communicating nonverbally.

"Well," said the tall agent with the Southern accent, "this sure is helpful. The research team is gonna wet their panties when they see this."

I heard a chuckle come from the short agent. "Yeah this is a good start to figure this afterlife shit out for good. Now what about him?"

"We already got our orders. He's coming with us," the tall agent replied.

"Like hell I am!" I yelled.

I turned toward the agents and tried to squirm away from the chair again. I was able to stand on my feet for a brief second before the two men grabbed me by my shoulders and slammed me to the ground. Now I was tied to the chair and laying on the carpet as these insane agents were pinning me down.

"Let me go, you sons of bitches," I yelled with my face smushed to the carpet. "You said I wasn't in trouble and you just wanted to ask questions."

"That's not exactly what I said," responded the tall officer who had his elbow pressed onto the side of my face. "I said we were here to ask questions but I didn't say that's ALL we were here to do. And you aren't exactly in trouble, as long as you comply. You know too much, Raymond. The outside world isn't safe for people who know or see too much shit. Especially things regular people have no business knowing about."

A moment later, the two agents grabbed me and my backpack and dragged me out of the room. They forced me out of the hotel and led me to a black SUV with no plates. They pushed me into the back seat and the hotel staff and other guests watched with wide eyes and bewilderment.

I kicked and tried to slide back out of the car when the short agent grabbed me by my neck and pushed my head to the side. I watched out of the corner of my eye as he pulled out a syringe.

"Be still," commanded the agent.

"Fuck you," I spat with my face pushed against the car seat. A second later I felt a sharp prick in the side of my neck and I lay there as my body felt limp and my eyes began to close. I felt my body and my brain shut down as the agent slammed the car door.

That was all I could remember before waking up again. I still didn't even know which country I was in. I wasn't sure if I was still in Greece, or somewhere else, but I did know I was in some kind of a room. I looked around and noticed I was wearing a white shirt with white pants that had no pockets and I had white crocs on my feet. The floor was plain white and there were only three white walls in the room that were barely twenty feet in length and width.

In place of a fourth wall was instead a glass barrier. After regaining my strength in my legs and arms, I slowly stood up and walked over to the glass. Behind it, I saw a hall in which other rooms like mine were stacked on top of each other like tiles on a Rubik's Cube. Each room had a person who was also dressed in white that I assumed was put on us by whoever ran this place. Each of the people looked like they were trapped in their own enclosure.

I realized then, just like everybody else in this rigidly structured nightmare, I was a prisoner.

Each of the cells had a metal table in the center with a bowl in the middle. In one of the rooms, I saw one prisoner, a young brunette with green eyes, staring at her bowl, and she began to sob and hold herself as if staring at the most terrifying thing imaginable. She started to back away only to be interrupted by a plain white wall. I watched in horror as the woman began screaming and scratching at the wall in a desperate, animalistic attempt to get away from whatever was in the bowl. I almost hurled and turned my attention away when I saw bloody streaks from her fingernails as she raked them against the wall.

When I turned, I was facing another cell across from mine and I saw a middle-aged man with bruises on his arms and broken knuckles looking at the bowl in a hypnotic state. He snapped out of his daze and looked around as if he had just teleported in there. After pacing around the room he looked around and yelled, "Hello! Where am I? How did I get here?" Then he looked at his arms and bloody knuckles with a face full of confusion and asked, "Who am I? What am I?" A moment later, he drew his attention back to the bowl as if he had just noticed it for the first time. When he drew closer to it, he peered down into it with the same exact hypnotized stare as he had previously. I could've sworn I saw a web of drool slowly drip from his bottom lip as he stared down at the bowl absentmindedly.

My attention was drawn away when I heard someone screaming. I looked around and noticed another cell that was on top of the cell that held the confused man. In this one, there was a heavyset woman huddled in the corner. She was screaming and yelling in a foreign language, as if begging for mercy. It sounded like she was yelling and praying in Spanish. When I saw what she was looking at, I almost shit my pants. Sprouting from the bowl in her cell was a tall vortex of fire that twirled furiously toward the ceiling. The inferno was tall, but not tall enough to singe the ceiling. I thought I could hear the flame roaring and yelling in another language at the woman. It didn't sound like Spanish, but it damn sure wasn't English either. Whatever it was, it sounded ancient with a heavy dialect that made my heart race.

After seeing that, I backed away from the glass. I didn't want to see anymore of whatever the hell was going on in those cells. Who's controlling this prison? Why were we in these cells? And what did they put in those bowls that were terrorizing these prisoners?

I saw something shimmer from the corner of my eye. I slowly turned and saw a bowl sitting on a metal table in my cell. Was it always there or did it just materialize from nothing? I felt a compelling urge to approach it. As I did, I noticed a strange yet familiar movement inside.

The bowl was full of a pitch-black liquid that bubbled and hissed. A small discharge of vapor came out each time one of the bubbles popped and dissipated. The unforgettable smell of sulfur and decay rose up to my nostrils, almost making me gag. Then it hit me. I thought back to what Gallow$84 said about the five rivers that lead to Hades: Styx, the river of unbreakable oath; Cocytus, the river of lamentation; Acheron, the river of woe; Lethe, the river of forgetfulness; and Phlegethon, the river of fire. I looked back at the other prisoners who were being tortured by the bowls in their cells. All of the bowls were somehow carrying the substance that streamed from the five rivers. I then understood why it was so rare for anyone to survive the Gates of Hades and return. Even the ones that survived the trip didn't return; they were all sent here, to whatever this place was.

My thoughts were interrupted by a coarse whisper coming from the bowl in front of me. Then that whisper was joined by a dozen others like a mournful chorus. A few minutes later I stood in front of the bowl with my hands over my ears, trying to block out the voices that were forcing their way into my brain.

"It's your fault! Die! You're nothing! You abandoned your wife in that cave, you coward! Misery and hell fire is more than you deserve." The voices continued to say random and degrading things to me, things that no one would know unless they actually looked inside my memories and my deepest insecurities. There were so many of them that I had to back away, but as I did, I found myself trapped in a corner of that goddamn room. Whatever was happening in this place was diabolical and horrendous, and I knew those asshole agents who kidnapped me had something to do with it. I knew I had to find answers for why we were all here and how to escape from this madhouse. But for now, I had to remain strong.

I kept the image of Charlotte in the front of my mind as the black fluid continued to talk to me. I remembered the promise I made to her soul when I left the cave, and I used that to keep myself from becoming a victim to whatever entity was in that bowl. I couldn't let the Waters of Woe or the Gates of Hades control me, I had to resist the wicked forces that haunted me. The River and the Gates both had a taste of me, and they wouldn't stop tormenting me until I returned.

www.ingramcontent.com/pod-product-compliance
Lightning Source LLC
Chambersburg PA
CBHW030607130626
46552CB00006B/2691